The Men in
the Woods

The Men in
the Woods

Mark C. Eddy

IGUANA

Publisher: Meghan Behse
Editor: Holly Warren
Proofreader: Lee Parpart
Cover design and illustration: Angela Vaculik (AGP Studio)

978-1-77180-308-3 (paperback).
978-1-77180-309-0 (epub).
978-1-77180-310-6 (Kindle).

This is an original print edition of *The Men in the Woods*.

This book is dedicated to my sister, Lori. The world needs more writers like you.

Prologue

November 1942

Krupp heard the cries growing louder. A bell rang. Krupp worried about how he appeared to the motorists who had stopped their vehicles. He hastened away from the nightmare that unfolded behind him and glanced towards the row of cars but didn't see anyone looking his way. All eyes were on the blaze.

He looked back on the chaos behind him. The fire had spread faster than he had expected. The hostel was completely engulfed. Columns of smoke rose from the windows. Flames licked out, tasting the cold night air. To his surprise, some of the building's occupants were still alive — choking, charred, but escaping. *Would they survive?*

As he rounded a street corner, he caught a boy staring at him, sensing he didn't belong. The boy said nothing, but his gaze lasted too long for Krupp's liking. Krupp stared back and tried to speak to the boy with his eyes. His stare said, *Look away now and forget that you ever saw me.*

The boy read the message and dropped his gaze. When he passed the boy, Krupp touched him on the shoulder — a gesture that also carried a message. The boy knew that Krupp *could* strike him if he wanted.

A few steps farther, Krupp took a sharp right turn. He dodged through a narrow passage between two row houses that lined the downtown streets. At the end of the passage was his car and, with it, his means of escape. Soon he would be back at his forest camp, his mission complete. Almost.

Chapter 1

Frank's head banged against the window. His eyes sprang open. Passengers sitting near him gave concerned looks. Embarrassed, he gestured that he was fine. The airplane pitched back and forth a few more times before it settled.

Frank hated to fly, and he was trapped until the plane landed. He had suggested to his commanding officer that he travel by ferry instead. His CO insisted that flying would expedite his assignment, and the Royal Canadian Air Force wanted this case closed as soon as possible.

He saw only grey below him. Clouds mingled with spots of the steely Atlantic — a great sea creature that had come to the surface to show everyone how goddamn ugly it was.

Finally, a break in the cloud cover gave him a wide view of the ocean. It was his first experience with the Atlantic. The closest thing he could compare it to was Lake Ontario back home. He wondered if Newfoundlanders made the same comparison when they travelled up his way.

The young woman next to him watched him with concern. She was probably worried about that hit he took to the head. He recalled the conversation they had had during the beginning of the flight. Didn't she say she was a secretary getting transferred to Newfoundland?

He straightened up and wiped the sleep from his eyes. He thought of something charming to say, but all that came out was, "Are we in St. John's yet?"

"No, sir. We should be there in twenty minutes."

"Oh, thanks. It's just as well that I woke up from my nap then." He tipped the brim of his service cap to her. He was surprised when she replied with a suggestive smile. He gave an appreciative glance at her legs and smiled back. *Women are suckers for a man in uniform*, he thought.

Frank didn't have to wear his uniform on this assignment, but he thought it would be best to have it on while travelling. He had heard that Newfoundlanders could be uneasy about foreigners. These days, he couldn't blame them. The uniform signalled that he was an ally. Once they saw he played on the same team, surely, they would warm up to him.

Frank collected the briefcase that had been thrown to the plane's floor. With twenty minutes before landing, he had just enough time to reread the files prepared for him by the intelligence service. The documents all began with the same background information that he and everyone else in the RCAF already knew but was required in every full report anyway.

Hitler's war machine had been rampaging across Europe since the war began. France and Poland fell in a matter of weeks. Norway lasted only two months. Great Britain had withstood invasion — barely — but whether Britain could successfully invade continental Europe was a completely different matter. On the positive side, the Soviets and the Americans were now fully involved and fighting on the right side.

The files stated in no uncertain terms that the Germans were inflicting heavy losses on the Allies in the Battle of the

Atlantic. The number of ships, both naval and merchant, sunk by German U-boats was staggering. One document stated that by the end of 1939, Hitler's sea wolves had sunk over two hundred ships in the battle. It was all part of Germany's strategy: Great Britain was an island power, and the British wouldn't last long if supplies — fuel, food, weaponry — weren't arriving at its docks. If marine shipping could be severed from the island, then Great Britain would be starved into submission.

In planning this strategy, it didn't take Germany long to realize that Newfoundland could play a major part in it. It was the farthest point east in North America. How could it not be a key platform for launching operations?

And what role would Canada play in the fight? The nation had been ill-prepared when the war started. There weren't enough men in the military. There weren't enough weapons and equipment either. The gear that Canada did have was outdated for the most part — a generation behind that of its stronger allies and of Germany. The result was that Canada's military almost exclusively comprised novices as green as shamrocks, and every soldier, whether recruited or seasoned, was trained on old machinery meant for fighting the last war.

To make matters worse, Canada's men and materials were being spread too thin. German U-boats had already penetrated deep into the nation. In May, just six months earlier, a U-boat crawled its way into the Gulf of St. Lawrence and sunk a pair of steamers. There was now a great threat to Canada's local shipping in the Gulf, and possibly in the St. Lawrence River. This new hazard directed precious allied warships and men away from the Atlantic convoys.

Frank breezed over the pages and saw unsubtle finger-pointing and many paragraphs about the dire naval situation being caused by a lack of coordination and communication between the Allies.

He doubted the public knew the extent or gravity of the situation. No newspaper in the country would dare criticize the military during wartime, but Frank, a military man, had the inside scoop.

Word travelled between navy and air force personnel. Frank had heard from more than one sailor that Canadian ships generally had lousy radar and sonar, weak guns, inaccurate compasses, and a whole slew of other insufficient and broken equipment.

The Allies were clearly suffering, but there was another common theme in the files: the northeastern Atlantic had seen some victories in the last few months. The Allies might have started turning things around. Allied warships were protecting convoys better than before, and air patrols out of Nova Scotia and Newfoundland were destroying enemy submarines. It looked like Canada was getting its act together — its industrial base, well-educated populace, and wealth of natural resources were finally making gains. The nation was still well behind its allies and enemies, but the Canadian military was shaping into a force to be reckoned with. Cross-training and intelligence-sharing with American and British allies were also helping Canada catch up.

Frank cursed under his breath. If only Canada had built up and maintained its military after the Great War ended. Instead, it dwindled in size and sophistication for over twenty years and was in a pitiful state when war broke out in 1939. If the military had been kept war-ready, it wouldn't have had to scramble to get up to speed when the Second

World War broke out. Frank could only hope that his nation learned this hard lesson. In future years, perhaps Canada would be better prepared, but what were Canada and its allies to do now?

Frank shuffled through the heap of files in his lap. They all finished with the same point: The Battle of the Atlantic could go either way — it was too early to tell for certain. Frank rolled his eyes whenever he read that. The last thing Canada needed were fence-sitting analysts afraid of giving firm answers.

Frank closed his case folder and rubbed his brow. He felt a headache building in the left side of his forehead. He wished he had more information about Newfoundland's intelligence capabilities. What kind of intelligence network did the local police have? He knew that the Newfoundland Constabulary had a department that specialized in intelligence-gathering, but Frank couldn't see a handful of small-city cops being up to the task. He grumbled. Before the war, they were probably handling motor vehicle accidents and hosting the occasional visit from the British royalty.

The plane jerked. Frank hated flying, and the crappy weather compounded his fear. Then a hard landing — so rough he cursed aloud. He thought the plane would skid off the runway. The pilot kept it under control, and Frank let out a relieved sigh. He was embarrassed for losing his calm.

The woman sitting next to him flashed him a smile as he exited, and said "I hope you had a nice flight." Did she have terrible hearing or was she just pretending to have not heard him swearing during touchdown?

"It wasn't so bad, thanks to the lovely company." He winked. "Though, the next time I have to come to this island, I'll swim."

Chapter 2

The submarine sliced through the water. Under what little moonlight there was, Wolfram saw sea spray blowing over the bow. He wasn't a sailor, but he knew that it was best to sail the U-boat at night. It could stay surfaced and move twice as fast than when submerged, but it would still have the cover of darkness. The wind battered the small part of his face left exposed. Gusts forced him to squint and the night's shadows obscured his surroundings. There wasn't much there anyhow — just the drowning bow ahead of him.

Wolfram leaned against the edge of the conning tower. He watched the ocean and evaluated the voyage up to that point.

The autumn weather had been more than agreeable. There was little ice to concern them, and not much stormy weather, and calm, open seas had helped them move quickly.

Fortunately, there had been some convenient fog banks along the way. One of the boat's drawbacks was that it could stay underwater for only about a day before it had to surface to recharge its batteries. This was when a U-boat was most vulnerable to detection and attack. The fog — like night's darkness — gave them the cover they needed.

Wolfram felt an arm brush against his, reminding him he wasn't alone on the conning tower. He stood next to the U-boat's captain. So important was his mission that the U-boat was commanded by one of Germany's aces, Captain Baumbach. He was young, but Baumbach seemed to know his business well. The telltale sign was the way the crewmen interacted with him — respectful but relaxed. They trusted him to bring them back to port.

Wolfram knew that the German navy, the Kriegsmarine, resented its precious submarines being used to insert teams of operatives when they could be out killing merchant vessels. Yet the captain never griped to Wolfram about that.

He leaned towards the captain, careful not to let go of the tower's railing. "How fast do you think we are going?"

"Here on the surface, we are close to our top speed of a little over eighteen knots. We are making good time now!" the captain hollered back. "You understand, if we left a couple of months later, we would have to contend with the ice and fog fouling the navigation and perhaps even causing a collision with another vessel. But now? It's easy sailing now, with little to obstruct us."

"Our luck has held so far, has it not? It feels like we left France months ago. Still, we've had no contact with the enemy."

Baumbach chuckled. "Yes, but we have had no contact with our base in France either. We do not send any radio transmissions that could be used to locate the vessel's position, and we try to surface only at night. I have not lived this long by being careless."

The captain took a drag from his cigarette, exhaled. The smoke vanished into the Atlantic's gale. "You see, Wolfram, it is not so much about luck as it is cunning and good tactics. The British navy is focused on escorting convoys of merchant ships across the Atlantic to keep Great Britain supplied with goods. Anti-submarine warfare is a distant second priority. Thus, if you avoid the convoys, then you avoid the British and American warships."

"Ahh, I see. Yes, that makes sense. Is there any Canadian navy we need to worry about?"

Baumbach smiled. "The Canadian navy? I don't think we have much to fear. Their crews are inexperienced. Their ships, such as they are, are too few. Watching the Canadians try to secure the shipping lanes to Europe is like watching a Dutch boy try to plug holes in a dyke while we Germans bring a sledgehammer to the damned thing." The captain chuckled. "And one does not need to be a code breaker to know that the British are frustrated with their North American ally."

"I've heard that the Canadian navy is becoming better at submarine hunting." Wolfram said.

The end of the captain's cigarette flared, and Wolfram could see the captain was smiling. "Oh, you have done some research. I like that! I bring so many soldiers onto my vessel who don't know the bow from the stern. It's nice to find one that prepares. Well, what you said was true. The Canadians are making improvements in the new kind of warfare. They have been acquiring more ships for the purpose. Small, fast crafts outfitted for submarine detection and elimination. Destroyers and corvettes are preferred, but the government is not averse to buying commercial vessels, like little yachts, and arming those. They are not very seaworthy vessels that can be relied upon to stay afloat in a deep-ocean storm, but they are more than suitable for coastal patrol and guarding ports."

"Do you have any other worries, Wolfram? I'd be happy to answer any questions or concerns."

"Thank you, Captain. This will be the first time my team has been inserted into an operations zone by sea.

Once we near the coast, how much do we have to worry about getting spotted?"

"Not much. The waters off Newfoundland are lightly patrolled. Plus, the island has almost no coastal defences. There is an English saying about a picture being worth a thousand words. Come with me. I want to show you something."

The two men climbed down the tower's internal ladder to the vessel's control room. The captain spread a map across a small table. Wolfram didn't need the captain to explain that the map displayed the eastern coast of Newfoundland. He had studied the coastline enough before boarding the U-boat.

"I'm delivering you to a place called Conception Bay," the captain said. "Here, on the Avalon Peninsula." He pointed to a spot on Newfoundland's east coast. "I've never sailed in the bay myself, but from the maps and charts, it doesn't look like there is much in the way of reefs or sandbars for us to worry about. Also, our past operatives in Newfoundland have informed us that there is not much in the way of coastal guns along the shore."

Wolfram could see how close it was to St. John's. Even a civilian could hike to the city in two days, and his men were far from being civilians.

"I will land you there on the first night we have good cloud cover and a calm sea, when there are no big waves," the captain said.

"Big waves might help to conceal us."

"They might help to drown you in the surf too. Trust me. This may be your first insertion by sea, but it is not mine."

Wolfram conceded with a nod. "Would you mind if I take that map back to my quarters? I would like to study it in more detail."

"No trouble at all," the captain said. "Please, continue with your research!"

Wolfram rolled up the map and tucked it under his arm. He crossed the room to the doorway and turned to the captain. "We will speak again soon. And soon after that, I am sure you and your crew will be heading home, where I am equally certain a well-deserved feast and some shore-leave await. For my team, our ordeal is only getting started."

The captain laughed. "No, I think not. The Kriegsmarine did not send us across the Atlantic to only deliver you. We are to stay close to the coast in order to extract you too — after you successfully complete the mission, of course. We are then to head south and ravage the Canadian coast for several more weeks. Great Britain does not die by itself, Wolfram."

"So, that's the plan — to wait off Nova Scotia, or somewhere like that, for a choice target to come along?"

"Trust me, it is much more complicated than that," Baumbach said. "We rely on intelligence concerning Allied ships. One of the best ways to gather it is to monitor civilian radio transmissions from broadcasting stations on shore. Occasionally, a newsman will accidentally expose some details. He will give away a date here or a ship's name there … each part is a piece in a puzzle."

"And it's your job to put them together, yes?"

Baumbach growled, "I admit that is a frustrating and tedious part of the job, but it is far from the worst."

Wolfram laughed, and the captain joined in.

The captain continued, "It may help to tell your men that this U-boat is a Type IX. It is more spacious and comfortable than the older model that I and many of the crew have served on. It is better armed and protected too. That may ease complaints from your men, and there are always some complaints, I don't care how good of an officer you are."

"Thank you for informing me, Captain. I will be sure to share those points with them." The two men saluted, and Wolfram took his leave.

***

Wolfram sprawled along his bunk, using his coat as a pillow. His conversation with the captain confirmed what Wolfram believed: that young ace knew what he was doing. He was glad Baumbach had shared more details about his part of the operation. His remarks were sensible, well presented, and reassuring. The Allies would try to protect their convoys while the submarine slipped past. Wolfram's team was safe for the time being.

He knew that once he reached shore, however, it would be another matter. Wolfram didn't agree with torching the hostel in St. John's. Staging it so close to his own mission alerted the authorities that the Germans were active in Newfoundland. Now he would have to execute his own mission in the face of their heightened readiness.

As for his men, he was still undecided about them. That was a bad position for any leader after an operation had already started.

His men were Brandenburgers, the elite force of the German army. And within the Brandenburgers, they were the *Küstenjäger*, coastal raiders trained specially by the German navy for operations like this one. After they had undergone group training in sabotage, demolitions, coastal operations, and a host of other skills, they appeared to be functioning as a team.

One issue lingered in Wolfram's mind, but he had no control over it at this point: He liked to personally select the members of his teams. There was a confidence that came from hand-picking them — a trust. This time, the members of his team were selected for him based on their linguistic skills, cultural knowledge, and ability to pass for regular North Americans.

The only one of his men he knew prior to the operation was Manfred Rudolph, the team's medic. The two served with each other before either of them was in the Brandenburgers.

And so, he now found himself at this strange pass: He was leading his team — a team he had doubts about — to an undoubtedly dangerous place.

Wolfram closed his eyes and yawned. He would have to make do with what he was given, just like everyone in the whole damn army these days.

Chapter 3

From the storage room, Beth could hear the phone ringing. She rushed to the store's front counter, but she was too late. It had to be Jack; he was the only one who called her after the store was closed.

"What on Earth does he want?" she whispered. It would be the second time he had called in the last twenty minutes. Ever since the accident, he had been playing the older brother role more intensely than ever.

She thought that whatever Jack wanted, it could wait. His overbearing concerns were a small matter next to the amount of inventory that needed to be unloaded, stocked, and catalogued.

At least she'd gotten the last of the boxes stacked. She tried to get rid of a lot of the merchandise in an end-of-season sale, but that hadn't worked out as she'd hoped. She needed the room for the winter merchandise that was just arriving. She saw a pile of it had tumbled across the floor from the store's back room and wondered where she would find room for it all.

First, she needed some medicine. She removed the ring box from under the counter. It felt less embarrassing to keep the medicine in the box than in a pill bottle. She opened the box, and using her left hand, shook out two painkillers. Everything had to happen with her left hand now; thankfully, she was slowly getting used to it.

She swallowed the pills with a glass of water that she now routinely kept under the counter. A bolt of pain struck below her shoulder blades. She winced. That's what annoyed her the most — how the little things that she once did effortlessly had become so difficult. Things like swallowing pills. She realized she had taken her mobility for granted. Now, formerly simple tasks were obstacles she needed to negotiate every day. How to get dressed using one hand, how to open the mail with one hand, how to cook with one hand — all were challenges that needed new techniques previously foreign to her.

She looked at her right arm. The hand's middle finger twitched, and she felt a tingle in one fingertip. It was one of the few occasions in the day when her arm's paralysis disappeared and she had a glimmer of hope that she would one day have full command of it again.

At least her arm never hurt like her back did. She looked at the ring box of pills and wondered if she would need to take painkillers for the rest of her life. A right arm that felt almost nothing and a back that was in constant turmoil — there was no fairness in that.

She let out a sigh and hated the sound of exasperation passing her lips. Just one more thing she couldn't control.

Beth wished she had someone to help her with the inventory. The store was a two-person operation. Her husband, Gerald, never helped to run the place anymore. *And to think, opening the enterprise was his idea.* That was just another unfairness to heap upon the growing pile in her life.

The Fit to Last was a hardware store on Duckworth Street, only a few hundred feet from the harbour. It catered to downtown residents doing small construction projects, like putting lovely little gardens in their backyards. The competing stores in the area were small compared to it. The Fit to Last carried the broadest range of products.

"Just like a carpenter's toolbox, a hardware store should be big but tightly packed with good stuff!" Gerald had said.

He always spoke about the store with such pride. *His* store. Beth knew how much elbow grease he had put into building the store. She knew because she had been with him the whole time, and no small amount of her own elbow grease went into it either.

She could thank her husband for choosing the store's product line. He had been convinced that selling expensive, top-quality goods was the right business approach. From pricey work boots to high-end plumbing tools, the store had it all.

"Beth, trust me. If I set up a hardware shop downtown, one that's selling top-quality gear, other hardware stores around with their shit gear won't be able to compete. We'll knock them out of the market! I know a lot of tradesmen who would be interested."

But they never came. The public found that the department stores around town sold cheap gear that served them just as well.

Now Beth stared coldly at the expensive shovels hung on racks next to overpriced axes. She scanned over to the rifles and shotguns that hung behind the counter. Those were late additions to the store's products. "A lot of people are scared these days. Scared that the Nazis might land over here one day. If we stock the place with guns, they'll sell like hotcakes!"

To date, they had sold only a single shotgun. It was a birthday gift for a teenage boy. He returned it to the store the next week. That was just another thing for her and Gerald to fight over.

The low sales deepened them in debt that they now had to pay back to the bank, plus what they owed to *both* sets of parents. Inviting them to Sunday dinner as a ploy to ask for another loan became too common.

She stopped trusting Gerald six years before when he withdrew all of the money from the bank account without telling her. The money went towards buying shares in a small cement manufacturing company on the island's west coast. Gerald had received a "great investment tip." The company was set to announce its new contract to supply cement to big budget government projects. A battle over property rights within the company surfaced. First, the contract froze; then the company folded.

"How the hell could you do this? That money was supposed to be for us when we get older!"

"I knew that if I told you, you would have tried to talk me out of it," Gerald said.

"You're damn right I would have. Now we're out hundreds, and we have nothing to show for it, Gerry."

Trust lost is always the first step towards love lost. The last five years had been a nightmare. Her resentment and anger led to other problems in the home, which led to his infidelity. He agreed to speak with their reverend about it, but the sessions backfired. The counselling only provided more topics for them to fight over.

War broke out, and business started booming. The Fit to Last had a steady stream of customers from opening to closing each day. They couldn't set a box of nails on a shelf without someone buying it within an hour.

But it was too late. Beth's marriage to Gerald had already soured. Some relationships can't be mended, no matter how good the money gets. Too many tears had been shed over too many hurtful things said.

Beth barely had time to wonder what the next step would be when Gerald threw her out of their house. The same house they once thought they would grow old in together. Her heart broke. When he added that his new "lady friend" would be moving in to take her place, she almost had a breakdown.

Her faith in God sustained her. Well, God and her brother. Jack let her move in with him until she could get settled someplace else.

By the time she finished her work at the store, it was 7 pm. It never took her as long as she expected, but it was long enough. Her back was knotted into painful coils of muscle. She wasn't due for another painkiller, but she was forced to take one. She swallowed and prayed that the extra medication would make all the difference, that that night's sleep would be better than the last.

Beth went to the store's office in the back to fetch her purse. She caught a glance of herself in the room's mirror. With her hair tied back in a bun, she had a full view of a face that begged for sleep. Thankfully she also took notice of the brown coat she was wearing. It was long, hanging below her knees, with the Red Cross badge sewn on its left breast. She remembered, with great regret, her promise to deliver supplies to the Red Cross's hostel after she finished work. Her day wasn't finished yet. She groaned.

Beth's injuries never stopped her from doing her part for the Empire like any other good British subject. Beth had been volunteering with the Canadian Red Cross ever since it had opened operations in the city. Each Saturday and Sunday, she volunteered at the Cross's warehouse in the city's Battery area, which lay along the waterfront. She was well-suited there. Tracking inventory was easy for her, since she always had a head for numbers. Also, it wasn't that different from her regular job at the store.

To keep the volunteer work interesting, she also assembled what were referred to as comfort bags, which were given to the survivors of U-boat attacks after they were rescued and brought into St. John's. Each bag looked like a small black pillow. It contained chewing gum, chocolate, shoe polish, socks, and — of course — cigarettes. What better way to show the unfortunate and battered survivors that the people of this great city cared for their well-being than by giving them a pack of smokes to calm their nerves? Each bag held everything Beth felt a survivor needed to feel better. Well, almost everything.

She remembered the first time she saw the survivors. It was a year ago, when a rescue ship pulled into port, carrying the survivors from a passenger ship that had been torpedoed. The survivors had been drifting in open lifeboats for days. The merciless Atlantic had taken its toll. By the time a passing freighter spotted one of the boats, some of its occupants had died. Others needed to have their frost-bitten limbs amputated. A shiver climbed up the back of Beth's neck. She wished never to see people so desperate ever again. But after seeing them, how could she do anything but want to help?

With the Red Cross, she worked just as hard as any other woman — even with only one good arm. She certainly did her share of sleepless nights assembling those comfort bags. She enjoyed that part. By placing each item inside a bag, it was as if she was sending a small, tacit message to some unfortunate person that they were loved, even by a stranger.

Beth liked the work so much that she even took some of it back to her home or to the store and worked on the bags when time permitted.

She grumbled and stared at a huge bunch of comfort bags sitting between a stack of wool army blankets and an unfolded pile of donated clothes. All the supplies needed to be brought to the hostel tonight. She bent and picked up a stray tube of toothpaste that must have fallen out of an open bag and placed it inside.

To make matters worse, she would have to face the other ladies at the hostel. For the most part, they were classy women, some from the city's most reputable families, and they wanted to do their share for the war effort just like Beth. She couldn't fault them for any of that. And they *were* polite to her. But they pitied her and got so awkward when she was around. A week ago, she had heard a group of the other volunteers giggling about the weekend dance at Fort Pepperrell, the American army base. They laughed about their servicemen sweethearts. They debated who they thought was more attractive — the Americans with their perfect teeth, the British with their hypnotic accents, or the Canadians whose manners never failed them.

None of the women asked Beth for her opinion. And none invited her to the dance. It wasn't that she wanted to go to the dance. As a jilted woman in her 30s, she felt she was too old to be kicking up her heels alongside a bunch of young girls who were barely out of their books. What bothered her was that the girls never invited her because that was how *they* saw her. To them, she was just an old pile of broken feelings that was cast away by her husband.

Beth made her way to the front door, and turned back to give the store one last, worried look. With a click of the lights, the boxes of brass fittings, coils of electrical cords, and every other damn thing that wasn't hers vanished. And Beth wondered when the bad luck would end.

Chapter 4

Frank's plane hadn't landed in St. John's, exactly. It had landed in Torbay, a small town about ten miles north of the city. The Royal Canadian Air Force had built an airfield, and while it accommodated bombers, fighters, and patrol planes, it also served the force's small passenger planes like his.

Leaving the airport, he found that the weather was nothing like what he had just left in Ontario. The wind battered against his right ear, making it difficult to hear a cab driver calling for him to climb into his taxi.

He looked skywards. In the distance, great beams of light danced about each other in a mantle of dark clouds. He guessed they were part of the city's defence forces, training against air raids. Or maybe they were just testing their spotlights. He was heading towards their source.

Driving to his hotel in downtown St. John's, Frank got his first close view of the city. For him, what stood out about St. John's was how old, shabby, and unattended everything looked. Vacant lots were resting places for shards of broken glass and abandoned furniture. Potholes cratered the roads. The sidewalks were veined with fissures where there should only have been slim cracks. Many of the concrete walls that he saw were in such disrepair that Frank was sure he could remove their exposed stones with his hands.

"Somebody needs to put some money into this city," he said to himself.

"Excuse me?" the cabbie said.

Frank realized too late that he had spoken aloud. "Sorry," he said. "I was just thinking that it would be nice if the government spent a little more money on the city's infrastructure."

"The Newfoundland government already spends everything that it has on St. John's."

Frank grimaced when he thought about the state of Newfoundland's other towns. He was about to ask but kept silent. He didn't want to be rude.

The city's scattered street lamps were the brightest lights around, but even they had been dimmed to comply with the mandatory blackout. From what he could tell, in this poor light, most of the streets were unpaved. Also, almost all the cars and trucks he saw were painted in drab army colours and emblazoned with military insignia. What few civilian vehicles there were, he assumed, belonged to well-off folks.

Frank stared at the rows of houses that lined the streets — wooden frame buildings, almost all three stories, with high windows. They were unlike homes he had seen back in Ontario — painted in outrageous pastels, creating a chain of rainbows. He smiled at the chaos of red, blue, purple, orange. Even in the dim light, it was still such a curious display. He wondered if the vibrantly coloured homes were the people's way of countering the dreary weather. Heavy shades, shutters, blankets, and drapes covered many of the windows — more reminders of the blackout.

Since most buildings were only a few storeys, the most prominent feature in the downtown was the giant Catholic cathedral that would have looked more at home in a centuries-old, European city than here. With its double towers, it crowned St. John's with a grace that was made all the more powerful by the city's otherwise modest skyline. Frank was sure that the building could be seen from every angle of the city. He noted that, if need be, he could use the cathedral as a reference point while navigating the city's winding streets.

The church bells rang. A funeral procession moved to the churchyard. It was late in the day for a funeral, but the war had a way of warping time. Half of the attendees wore civilian clothes. The rest were military men in dress. As the taxi rolled slowly through, Frank heard the minister raise his voice to be heard over the sounds of crying. The loudest mourner was a middle-aged woman in black. Frank wondered if it was her husband or her son who had been killed. Then the telltale husband stepped closer to the woman and placed his arm around her. The look of anguish on the man's face was unmistakable. Only the death of a child could twist a man's face that way.

Frank spied a handful of children playing marbles in front of the church. Kneeling around their game, they were oblivious to the ceremony transpiring behind them. Frank wished that it could always be that way for them. *Let them be spared the war's traumas and heartbreak.*

The taxi tumbled down the twisted streets towards the downtown area. It rolled past some Canadian soldiers manning their anti-aircraft battery. One soldier wiped down a cannon's ebony barrel while it pointed skywards. The other two had taken up seats on the circle of sandbags that formed the battery's perimeter.

How out of place the gun appeared on a commercial street lined with stores and shoppers. Nevertheless, someone had obviously decided that a stretch of sidewalk was a good site for an anti-aircraft cannon. And so, it was a new fixture — no different than a fire hydrant or park street bench.

From what he had read, the so-called "Friendly Invasion" of foreign soldiers had caused the city's population to leap from forty thousand to sixty thousand almost overnight. Frank saw streetscapes, made of mostly older buildings, punctuated by other structures that were obviously newly built — a guard post here, a barracks there, or a gun site like the one the taxi had just passed. These new constructions gave this aged city a contradictory impermanence, as if at any moment the Canadians and Americans might pack up their property and leave. Could it really happen that way? Could these armies pull down their tents and tarpaper huts, empty their sandbags, and roll away their mammoth cannons? And if it could unfold that way, what would the local people be left with besides the memories of the greatest magic trick that St. John's had ever seen?

The cab turned onto Water Street, where Frank's hotel was, and he saw a few department stores that looked worthy of the title. A movie house, playing the latest Hollywood releases, looked like it would suffice for entertainment. That is, if he had time to relax.

The taxi came to a stop in front of his hotel. After giving the driver a generous tip, he stepped out onto Water Street. He heard the clopping of horseshoes on cobblestones, along with the rumble of slow-rolling wagon wheels. Frank turned to see an overloaded wagon straining to carry its load of coal. Was it a man or a boy driving the wagon? It was impossible to tell. The wagoner's face was smudged with coal dust. The only feature Frank could make out was a pair of wet, bloodshot eyes. It reminded him that there were worse jobs to have than military policeman. Much worse.

The clanging streetcar ahead of him gave a better impression of newness than the coal wagon. The trolley was full of passengers, which made sense. Given the lack of automobiles that he had seen so far, he guessed that the city's residents relied heavily on the streetcar.

Once at the hotel, the desk attendant caught Frank's accent and mistook him for an American, despite the insignia on his uniform. Frank didn't correct him. Passing for an American when travelling outside of the country was just part of being Canadian. For Frank, it was a reminder of how the smaller nation below Canada always seemed to overshadow it.

When he signed in at the hotel, the desk's attendant gawked at his last name. "Frank Carousel? Carousel? Like at a fair! Well, you have no say over your family name, I suppose."

Frank replied with a polite smile, collected his bags, and wandered off to find his room.

He was relieved to close the door of his hotel room behind him. He was able to catch his breath, be himself. He tossed his service cap onto the room's only chair. It took only a second for his practised hands to unbuckle his white leather service belt that fit tight around his waist and strapped over one shoulder. The heft of his revolver caused the belt to plummet to the floor.

He rolled his shoulders and rubbed the back of his neck. Some exercise would work out the stiffness. Frank found that hotel rooms were the perfect place for calisthenics. A person didn't need much room or gym equipment for those.

First, he had to settle himself into his new accommodations. He placed his suitcase, unopened, in the closet. He then turned his attention to his only other luggage: a black leather carrying case. Frank unpacked its contents onto the dresser's top. He placed a compass next to maps of the city and Newfoundland. A small pair of binoculars came next. A notebook and a pair of pens followed, then a small camera with extra film completed the pile. He removed the folders containing his work files. Last, he took out a few short stacks of extra Newfoundland currency, in different denominations, to supplement the amount he already had in his wallet. He placed the money on top of the dresser. Frank was certain it would be safe to leave it lying in the open. No one would try to rob a military policeman.

He stripped off the rest of his uniform, and, in his boxers and undershirt, he set himself to his exercises. He hoped that the exercises would clear his mind. He had completed only twenty sit-ups before his thoughts drifted back to his assignment.

Four months earlier, there had been a fire at the Allied Servicemen's Club in downtown St. John's. That hostel had been catering to Allied servicemen, so most of the thirty-seven people who perished in the blaze were military.

An investigation couldn't determine the inferno's cause, but foul play was ruled out. In their concluding remarks, investigators suggested that the blaze could have been accidental. "Potentially started by something as simple as a burning cigarette," their report stated. Many people, including Frank, doubted that. It was too coincidental that the fire should strike a building filled with military personnel during wartime. As well, survivors reported that the doors had been barred from the outside, impeding their escape.

Twelve of the fatalities were members of the Royal Canadian Air Force, which meant the air force had to be involved in the follow-up investigations. It would appear improper if a dozen Canadians died and the investigation was left in the hands of foreigners. Furthermore, any chance of Canada staying out of the investigation had been erased by the tragedy at Dieppe. In August, five thousand soldiers, almost all Canadian, were defeated while raiding the German-occupied French port. Their goal was to make an amphibious landing on the beach, complete a few symbolic objectives, and then withdraw into the ocean only a few hours later. But more than three out of five men were killed, wounded, or captured. It was the most tragic day the Canadian military had ever seen.

Now, only three months after Dieppe, the Canadian public was pressuring the government to be more proactive and aggressive. Nobody on the home front wanted to see the nation suffer that enormous loss and then see the war effort left as it was. More needed to be done, and it needed to be done right. There was no chance the RCAF would stay out of Newfoundland after a suspicious fire had killed Canadian servicemen.

Frank suspected that his superiors were less concerned about the cause of the fire and more concerned with how things looked — making sure they showed up and were involved in the aftermath. Thus, he was dispatched to Newfoundland to examine the fire's site first hand and to review the facts of the case. He knew some of his peers believed he was sent to Newfoundland as a token gesture. He didn't believe it, and he had no intention of treating his assignment as a fool's errand. He planned to give the investigation more of his blood and sweat than he had ever given to any case. He felt he owed it to the victims.

Chapter 5

Just after finishing school, Frank left home to pursue a new life in Toronto. His mother was supportive. His father said he was a fool.

"Why run away to Toronto with no goal or plan?" his father asked. "Wouldn't it be better to work the farm with the rest of his family? Almost two hundred acres of farmland needs many hands to care for it."

Frank knew his father had a point. But he could no more resist the big lights and busy streets than he could persuade his father to come with him. By the time he had packed the suitcase his mother had bought for him, his father was begging him to stay.

Despite his family's worries, Frank had a good start in the city. It wasn't much, but he landed a job as a dishwasher at what may have been the greasiest diner on King Street.

That was where he met Joan. She was a red-headed beauty from Winnipeg who moved east to chase her dream of being a stage actress. Working at the diner may not have been her first choice, but she needed to pay the rent just like him or anyone else.

Frank, by contrast, couldn't have been more content with his life. Work in the city was no worse than that in the countryside, and there was always something exciting he could do in his free time. He especially enjoyed going to sporting events. Joan even got him interested in the theatre. She taught him how the costumes and props were made and how the stages were set. It fascinated him that the actors and actresses made it all look easy, while behind their flawless performances there was a whole machinery of rigging, lights, pulleys, and props.

Not long after they met, the acting company that Joan worked for went bankrupt. Frank had heard that as a rule, businesses selling luxury goods, services, and entertainment were the hardest hit by economic downturn. When it came time to save a few coins, trips to the theatre were among the first things to go. Even so, Frank was certain that with her looks and natural charm, she would find as many parts in as many plays as she could want.

Broke and with few career prospects, Joan moved to California to try her luck in motion pictures. Escorting her to the train station and saying goodbye was one of the hardest things he had ever done. He thought she would never stop crying. In a way, that helped him get through the whole experience. Comforting Joan took his attention away from his own feelings. Frank never heard from her again.

With Joan gone, he began to re-evaluate what was left of his life. He knew the job at the restaurant wouldn't satisfy him for much longer. He began looking into local trade colleges. After all, there was good money in being a tradesman. At the very least, he knew that his working a trade would do more to satisfy his father than his dishwashing ever would.

He registered for courses in a plumbing program, but his training was cut short. His cousin Lawrence showed up on his doorstep one morning to give him the bad news: His father had died of a heart attack. Frank hadn't had the chance to say goodbye.

Because Frank was the oldest son, the family's farm was left to him. After only one season of working the farm, he sold it, and thereby put his only sibling, Tom, out of work. He reassured Tom that the profits from the sale would be put to good use and that their futures were safe. He had a plan.

His childhood friend, Henry, had convinced Frank to invest the money in his business — a slaughterhouse and butcher shop. Frank didn't know anything about running either, but his friend assured him that he wouldn't need to do anything. He would be a silent partner and his friend would manage the business. The first year had gone well, and it seemed to Frank like a wise investment. But Frank never checked the books. He trusted Henry to handle running the business end to end.

The whole enterprise was in trouble even before Frank had joined. By the end of the second year, they were selling off the company's assets. Frank had squandered the family inheritance, and Tom was left jobless. Tom refused to speak to him, and the rest of the family seemed to only speak to him long enough to berate him. His heartbroken mother was the only one who was civil to him, but he didn't have the nerve to face her.

Given the situation, it was a surprise when the help he needed came from a family member. Lawrence, the same cousin who delivered news of his father's passing, was a bush pilot in the Royal Canadian Air Force. He mostly handled aerial surveys and cargo deliveries to remote areas in northern Ontario. Lawrence convinced Frank to sign up with the RCAF.

Lawrence wrote a letter of recommendation for Frank and told him what to say when he met with a recruiting officer. Just like that, Frank became a military policeman.

Frank wasn't nervous when the war started. He thought that being in the military police would save him from the front lines. He could do his part for the war effort but stay at a safe distance.

And he was right for the first few months. Frank had been stationed at a base on the home front, far away from the fighting. He was glad he hadn't been assigned to one of Canada's internment camps, where many people of Italian heritage had been sent. Since the war started, Canadian citizens were frightened of Axis sympathizers and fifth columnists walking among them. The fears were especially directed towards immigrant-rich cities like Toronto and Vancouver. Internment followed.

Frank sympathized with the prisoners. His own grandparents were Italian. His grandfather changed the family name from Caruso to Carousel, something he felt would be more pleasing to Canadian ears. Frank wondered how he would be treated today if his grandfather hadn't made that decision.

Frank spent much of his time guarding German prisoners. He had far less sympathy for these men. They had chosen to fight, but the interned civilians were unlucky victims of circumstance. For the most part, the German prisoners he had to guard gave no resistance. Although none of them were glad to be confined, they weren't eager to get back into the fighting either.

Every day, he fought his own battle against boredom. Most of his job involved searching for lost items and standing guard. His work was occasionally spiced up by a case of desertion or a punch-up between drunks. Once, an aircraft technician stole some beer from the canteen — he and the other police talked about it for two weeks. Another time, Frank worked with the civil police on a case of stolen property. That made him feel like a real cop. His job didn't leave him much to write home about (not that anyone cared to hear from him).

He eventually convinced his superiors to transfer him to the Service Police's Special Investigation Section. There he received advanced training in specialized crime prevention and investigation. Much of it focused on sabotage, espionage, and terrorism. Frank was happy with the change. The work was more demanding, and he felt this was the only way to stretch and grow in his career. He wasn't wrong.

His days of recording thefts at the canteen ended abruptly. For over a year, he had been waist-deep in real cases — violent assaults, arson, missing people — and there never seemed to be enough manpower for the growing number of cases.

One day, not unlike the day Frank received news of his father's death, his cousin Lawrence arrived on his doorstep to inform him of another tragedy. This time, it was Tom.

Frank received few details. There just wasn't much information available. Tom had also enlisted in the RCAF. He had been stationed in St. John's when the hostel he had called a temporary home burnt down. Tom was just one of the many servicemen killed.

Frank was furious when a report from the Newfoundland Constabulary stated that the cause of the blaze was undetermined and that it was possibly an accident. He had been following the investigation as closely as he could, so he knew there were others in the air force who didn't believe it either. He heard a rumour that senior command was considering sending one of its own to Newfoundland to either confirm or dispute the findings of Newfoundland's investigation. Frank pleaded with his superiors to choose him. He was afraid that his limited experience in the Special Investigation Section would disqualify him, but he guessed they didn't want a distraught policeman mixing with other military policemen on the base. As Frank saw it, it was just another place he wasn't wanted.

Chapter 6

After finishing his sit-ups and push-ups, Frank started a set of jumping jacks. He decided to skip supper. He figured it was good for his beltline to miss an occasional meal. He let out some gas and placed a hand on his belly. The exercise and the flight had made his stomach uneasy.

Once he finished with exercise, Frank grabbed his files from his case and sat in the room's leather chair. Reading at night always helped him fall asleep.

He had been provided with a special city map. It clearly delineated military installations. He was amazed at how much space was taken up by the various camps, bases, gun batteries, and other sites. If he were to guess, they collectively consumed one-fifth of the space within the city's limits. That didn't include the land beyond the city's boundaries, like the Torbay airfield on which he had just landed.

From the map, the city's most notable feature was, of course, the harbour. It was about seven hundred metres wide, two kilometres long, and shaped like a sock. The harbour's entrance was the opening of the sock, and a dockyard at the end of the harbour was the toe's tip. As expected, the harbour had been augmented with several new naval facilities and harbour defences.

He thumbed through the rest of the documents. No matter how many times he passed through them, Frank always lingered at the same one: a photograph of the hostel before the fire. He was so familiar with the picture from studying it so many times that he once tried to draw it from memory. His hand trembled as he held it.

The hostel was wide but only two storeys high. Its slanted roof and forest-green sides had no features to distinguish the hostel from the wooden buildings that surrounded it — that is, except for the plain, white sign near the main entrance's double doors. Even from a photograph, Frank could read it:

ALLIED SERVICEMEN'S CLUB

The City of St. John's Welcomes You!

The building looked to be neat and in good condition. It must have been one of the new buildings hastily erected to accommodate the legions of foreign servicemen who flooded into St. John's.

As if to prove his point, the photo showed a covered army truck parked next to the hostel's entrance. Three American troops leaned against it and smoked cigarettes. Frank squinted and leaned closer. He saw that one soldier was laughing while the other two exchanged suggestive smiles, like they were saying, "Can you believe this nutty asshole?" That thought made Frank grin, but his smile vanished when he wondered if these men had also died in the fire. Every time he stared at this photo, he saw something different, felt something different. Frank dropped the picture into the pile of documents.

He yawned and put all the files in his case. He had already done his homework, so what else was there to do besides get a good night's sleep? He shut off the light and climbed into bed.

Tomorrow would be Day One of his assignment, and he expected it would be busy. First, he would travel to an office of the Newfoundland Constabulary to meet his contact. He tried to remember the man's name — *Farrow? Farmer? Fowler?* That was it! Acting Sergeant Jack Fowler. Frank imagined Fowler would give some sort of orientation session once he arrived at his office. That suited Frank.

He worried about being perceived as the token representative sent by Canada to show its involvement — a symbolic gesture. Of course, this wasn't the case. Over a dozen Canadian servicemen couldn't die in a blaze without Canada insisting on doing its own investigation.

Frank yawned again and closed his eyes. Tomorrow, his assignment would really begin.

Chapter 7

The light in Wolfram's quarters flickered and dimmed. The U-boat had been experiencing some sort of power problem for the last hour. Wolfram closed his book. There was little point in trying to read in the poor light.

He lay the book on his bunk. *A History of Newfoundland* by Prowse. He had instructed his men to learn as much as they could about Newfoundland during their voyage to the island. For days, he had been filling his head with information on Newfoundland history, geography, and culture. Learning so much about the place had cultivated a fondness for it, and he thought he'd like to visit Newfoundland in better times.

Who knows? he thought. Perhaps in the next big war, Germany and Newfoundland will be on the same side.

Wolfram doubted it, but as his wife had been fond of noting, stranger things have happened. Hell, a lot of people thought that the current war would never happen at all.

He rose from his bunk to fetch himself some water. The submarine shifted, and he lost his footing. He landed against a wall of his small quarters. Wolfram hadn't gotten his sea legs yet.

Wolfram and his men were accustomed to hardships, but life on board a submarine brought a unique set of discomforts. To hell with what the captain had said about its improvements over an earlier model. They suffocated below deck in the stale air. They were assaulted by the constant smell of sweat, fuel fumes, and the pounding of machinery. None of his men had complained about the tight quarters, but he knew they were climbing the close walls to get the hell out of there. And he was too.

In fact, the greatest mishap in the journey thus far was a result of these poor conditions. One of Wolfram's men snuck up to the deck to grab a few breaths of fresh air during a change in the watch, and he was stopped by a crewman. One of Wolfram's clandestine operatives, a supposed master in stealth, couldn't even get some fresh air without being caught. Wolfram was embarrassed, especially in front of the ace captain. The operative's punishment was getting only half rations until they reached Newfoundland.

Wolfram grumbled, and for the hundredth time in the journey, wished for an airplane. If only there was a plane available that had the range to fly them to Newfoundland, then they wouldn't have to suffer in this giant tin can.

Despite all the U-boat's irritations, their voyage was still going well. The weather had remained excellent. The submarine spent a surprising amount of time on surface, where it could travel at a top speed of fifteen knots, roughly twice as fast as when submerged. Plus, the U-boat always seemed to pass one of those most convenient fog banks when one was needed for shelter.

And so, since leaving its base on the French coast, the U-boat had seen few dangers. Once, during the mid-ocean point of their voyage, they were spotted by a merchant ship. It fired a star shell into the sky to illuminate the ocean below, forcing the U-boat to crash-dive. Everyone on board prayed that they had escaped before being spotted again and that their coordinates had not been transmitted to enemy warships. Any moment, depth charges could plummet down from the surface above and send the U-boat to the bottom of the ocean. Hours passed. There was no further sign of the enemy. The relief was so great among the U-boat's occupants that Wolfram could almost feel the submarine itself let out a sigh and relax. Captain Baumbach's words were ringing true. The Allied warships were sticking to the convoys while the U-boat slipped past.

They had crossed paths with a fuel tanker heading towards Great Britain. How such a target ended up alone, they could only speculate. "It must have been a part of a convoy and became separated, probably by another attacking U-boat," the captain suggested. A less disciplined U-boat captain might have torpedoed it. Fuel was the most valuable commodity carried by the Allied ships. What a prize it would have been for Baumbach and his crew! Sinking it would have won them acclaim, medals, promotions, and shore leave. But the submarine ace wouldn't be steered from his mission. Wolfram counted himself lucky to be in good hands.

Wolfram unfolded the map that Baumbach had given him the previous day. Before his team landed in Conception Bay, he planned to draw it from memory. That was the best way to memorize every cove and outcropping of land in that bay.

He was interrupted by a knock at his door. Wolfram didn't recognize his visitor in the dim light until he noticed the ragged scar slanting down the man's chin. It was a souvenir from Crete. Fragments from a shell burst opened up the man's face, punching out some of his bottom and top teeth. Wolfram hadn't seen it, but he had heard the story from a couple other men.

Manfred Rudolph, one of his team's members and its medic, had brought his medical kit with him — the large pack hung from his right shoulder.

"Good evening, sir. You wanted to review some of the mission's medical supplies with me?" Manfred asked in English.

Wolfram looked at Manfred quizzically. The English caught him off guard, but Manfred was only getting into character. Wolfram was fluent in English; however, he couldn't speak it as convincingly as Manfred did — with no trace of his German accent.

Wolfram smiled and replied in English. "I see you are speaking only English to help with your cover."

"I'm sorry, sir. Should I go back to German?"

"Yes, a conversation in German would be most welcome. We are under the strictest orders to speak only English once we reach our destination, so any conversation we can still have in our native language should not to be missed."

Without asking permission, Manfred sat on the floor of the small room and leaned back against the wall. Wolfram wasn't bothered by Manfred's casualness. Formality was more relaxed among them than inside regular army units, especially when on a mission. The formality could slacken, as far as Wolfram was concerned, so long as the discipline didn't loosen with it.

"I had forgotten about asking you to visit my quarters for a discussion, but on second thought, perhaps it can wait. We can go over the operation in the morning at breakfast. Yes, that would be better. The rest of the team should probably hear what we have to say."

"Yes, sir. I wish you a good sleep," Manfred said, before turning to leave. Wolfram noticed that the mannerisms of his old ally were off. Manfred's shoulders slumped, and his movement was slow. The head that he once held up with such pride now faced downward. He was like a boxer trying to protect his chin.

"Manfred … what's wrong?"

"Nothing is the matter."

"I can tell when you are uneasy. I think we have known each other long enough that you can speak freely."

Manfred hesitated. Delayed responses from his men normally annoyed Wolfram, but not this time. He wanted to give Manfred all the time he needed to answer.

"I have a bad feeling about this mission, sir," Manfred said. "Conducting another operation in St. John's so soon after that hostel fire is a bad idea. The city will now have its guard up."

"I know. I have thought about it myself. But intelligence reports say that the city security is still weak. If so, then the Allies will soon learn what a daring enemy they face and how fatal a misjudgment they have made." He smiled.

"Intelligence has been wrong before, sir."

"I know that as well as anyone else in this army. But we pray that the information is accurate, or at least, not as bad as what the enemy is getting, and we go forward with that."

Wolfram could see that Manfred wasn't convinced. *He's probably wishing that he hadn't said anything to me*, Wolfram thought.

"Look, I know this one is risky, but I have good news. I was going to save it for tomorrow at breakfast to tell you and the rest of the men. After we get back to Germany, the team is being granted an entire month's leave."

Manfred's eyes brightened, and Wolfram knew that he had touched a pressure point. "Don't tell anyone tonight. I still want it to be a surprise."

"Very good. Thank you, sir." Manfred said, and his lips curved into a half smile.

"If there is nothing else, then I suggest we both get some rest."

"Yes, sir," Manfred said before he left Wolfram's quarters. Wolfram was content that he improved the disposition of at least one of his operatives. Of course, the line about the month's leave for everyone was a fiction. Wolfram did what a good operative does when he's in a bind: he lied. Once back in Germany, he would either secure the month's leave for real, or he would break the disappointing news to his men over many rounds of beer.

Wolfram didn't blame Manfred for his concerns about the mission's timing. If only that fool Krupp hadn't burnt down the goddamn hostel.

Nonetheless, Germany's high command had a growing concern that the Battle of the Atlantic may be slipping into the enemy's favour. Germany needed some solid wins to stop that from happening. Wolfram had been told that his mission, if successful, would be one of them. They needed to execute the mission now. And when senior command requested volunteers for a high-value mission, he didn't hesitate to raise his hand. Not this time. Not any time.

Wolfram sighed. The operation was in play, so whether it should have begun in the first place counted for little now. But there was still the issue of Manfred. What was to be done with him? Manfred was a good man and an excellent soldier — of these facts, Wolfram had no doubts. But still, Manfred had lost much of his fighting spirit after Crete.

Both men had fought in the Battle of Crete when the island fell to the Nazis. German paratroopers, the cream of the German military, suffered badly in order to gain that victory. Thousands of them landed on Crete. Some parachuted down to the island. Others landed in gliders. The British-led forces and Greek civilians poured gunfire into them before they could get free of their parachutes, disembark their gliders, or take cover and organize themselves. The hand-to-hand combat was brutal. Bayonets and rifle butts turned the Greek island into a scene reminiscent of an ancient battlefield, rather than modern warfare.

Manfred was one of the lucky few to suffer a light wound. He had been decorated for his actions on Crete. It wasn't much comfort after seeing two-fifths of his unit killed and another two-fifths wounded.

Even back in those days, Wolfram had heard many rumours about Manfred. The camp gossip said that before the war started, Manfred had a sweetheart who was an anti-fascist. He said her name was Sofia and that she and her family went into hiding when the war started. Manfred lost contact with her, but he believed they were found by the Gestapo and sent to a secluded camp. Wolfram had heard stories about the secret police's camps. He heard what happened to prisoners after they arrived. Thinking about it now made him shiver.

Wolfram figured that if that much of the story were true, it was best to believe Sofia was dead. The war had taught him to be a pessimist. And if Manfred were to learn that his darling Sofia was still alive, could he stand being apart from her? No, it was better to believe that she was gone from this terrible world and all its fire.

Wolfram had considered removing Manfred just before the mission started — some time away from the action to be with family and to rest might recharge him — but what would the other men think if Manfred took leave? More concerning, what would High Command think? The last thing Wolfram wanted was for High Command to review any of his men and discover rumours of a girlfriend who sided with the Allies. Even if the rumours were untrue, they might still be enough to land the remarkable young soldier in prison.

Thinking about Manfred's private life turned Wolfram's thoughts to his own. He rolled up his right shirt sleeve. On the inside of his forearm was a tattoo of three sparrows — a big one and two little ones. He wanted a picture to remind him of his wife and daughters while he was away from home. A photograph seemed like too much of a security risk. It would be just one more thing for a captor to use against him during an interrogation, or one more thing he might drop in a place where he wasn't supposed to leave anything behind.

Wolfram ran his finger across the tattoo. It stopped on the big sparrow. Johanna was born in Augsburg, in the Bavaria region of Southern Germany. Augsburg was a fine old city — a wonderful place to fall in love. It was where he met and fell for Johanna, but it's also where he fell for Germany's rich history. The love he found in Augsburg, for Germany, drew him to army life. He had often told Johanna as much. He would ask her how anyone could grow up in a place like Augsburg and not be enchanted by the military and its traditions. In response, she would always laugh and tell him that he hated war, but she promised she wouldn't tell the other officers.

Johanna and their daughters, Adela and Ilyse — his "three girls" — lived in the Ruhr valley. The Allies knew the region as Germany's workshop. Its manufacturing was vital to the war effort, so it was a prime target.

When he received the news that his family was killed in one of the Allies' early air raids on the Ruhr, he sobbed until he was hoarse, and he didn't care who the hell saw him.

He stopped and rolled down his sleeve. He told himself, as he had so many times before, that no matter what came next, he had to see the mission through. All his work, his losses, and all of Germany's losses couldn't be for nothing.

Wolfram grunted and tucked away the map that he had been studying before Manfred's visit. He spread across his bunk and used his coat as a pillow. There would be plenty of time for musing on romance and family later. As for Manfred, he would keep a close eye on him. If need be, he'd have the other men watch him as well. He would devote further thought to Manfred once he was rested. After all, they still had several hours to go before reaching Newfoundland.

Chapter 8

From the deck, Wolfram could make out a coal-black sky against a coast that was just a shade lighter. St. John's and its surrounding area were under a blackout order. The Newfoundlanders worried about the city's lights silhouetting ships near the shoreline, making them easy targets for nighttime U-boat attacks. They were smart to be afraid, considering his own U-boat had crept into Conception Bay this very night.

Wolfram had already decided to count the blackout as an advantage for his team. The more darkness they could wrap themselves in, the better.

He had accomplished the first part of his mission: getting his team to the Newfoundland coast. The team was anxious, but Wolfram could tell that each of its members was glad to be rid of the U-boat and the discomforts of its interior.

The operatives loaded themselves into a set of inflatable rafts. Captain Baumbach stood on the deck and pitched in to help with the departure.

There was no talking allowed during this part of the operation, so he only shook Wolfram's hand and nodded a farewell. Wolfram reciprocated before descending into a raft and grabbing an oar.

The next phase of the insertion went perfectly. They landed during the rising tide, with the waves helping to pitch them further into the beach. As well, the team landed where it had planned. That in itself was a noteworthy accomplishment for a mission like this. Members of the crew accompanied Wolfram's team, and after helping them to unload, rowed the rafts back to the submarine to avoid detection.

Baumbach had landed the operatives on the coast during a cloud-filled night. Wolfram looked skywards. He couldn't see the moon or any stars. Though they were on the coast, Wolfram couldn't feel a breath of wind. The waters at his back were calm. He listened to the waves wash onto the rocks behind him. And when those waves receded, the rocks clacked and crackled as they rolled backwards into the ocean. Its rhythm filled his ears. *Wash. Crackle. Wash. Crackle.* A sigh of relief passed his lips. He had landed his men safely, and in doing so, fulfilled a big promise.

From everything he had read, Newfoundland's shore was not normally this tranquil. He wasn't sure if the stillness was a good omen or a bad one. Then he shook the superstitions from his mind and set himself back to the task of marshalling together his men. The team ran towards a short, timber railway bridge that ran adjacent to the shoreline.

As soon as they took cover under the bridge's beams, a train crossed over. They watched it pass through the cracks above them. Wolfram leaned against a beam and let the passing train send vibrations down his back.

Wolfram knew what they were thinking. *Did anyone aboard that train see them?*

No, Wolfram thought, in the darkness of the moonless night, with the train travelling as fast it was, surely not. Surely not.

The operatives said nothing. They only waited and watched Wolfram for his next signal.

This gave Wolfram a moment to check his men, again. Little light was available, but they looked convincing enough. They had switched their German-issue firearms for American ones. They wore low-cut, American-issue army boots. Black, wool knit hats topped each head. Each operative wore olive coveralls with many pockets — the same sort of coveralls so many American soldiers wore. Wolfram knew that each man had done his best to complete his disguise — down to the US bills they carried in their wallets and photos of fake sweethearts and wives next to the cash. Underneath, each man wore civilian clothes, in case he had to switch out of his Yankee disguise. Wolfram nodded in reassurance to himself. If they were exposed, it wouldn't be due to unconvincing appearances.

Thirty minutes passed. It was a long time for a team to stay put after insertion. A young couple, enjoying an evening stroll along a footpath, came into sight. Wolfram's men watched them from the bridge's shadows, clinching their guns and waiting to see if they would need to silence the couple. Wolfram shook his head. His team wouldn't announce its presence over two lovebirds spending some time together.

The pair stopped long enough for the man to skim some rocks across a small freshwater pond near the bridge. His sweetheart smiled and cheered him on. They finally left, unaware of the violent men who lay in the shadows not a hundred feet from them. Wolfram was thankful for that. Killing non-combatants disgusted him.

Finally, Wolfram saw his subject approach. Frederick Krupp emerged from the line of pines to Wolfram's right.

Like Wolfram's team, this operative was staying in the shadows. Wolfram did not flash him a signal. Instead, he trusted that Krupp would come to their planned meeting place. A moment later, the operative was jogging towards him. Once he arrived, Krupp settled on the bridge's concrete base, smiling at the men. He wasn't one of them, but he didn't need to be for them to be overjoyed, and they smiled back. He was a fellow German soldier ending his mission and beginning his journey back to the Fatherland. Frederick had been operating in Newfoundland for two months. That was longer than many operatives would have endured, and Wolfram respected Krupp for that.

Wolfram finally broke the group's silence and greeted Krupp in English.

Still smiling, Krupp replied with a flawless American accent, "Ahh, you don't need to be reminded to switch to English while over here, do you? Good. That's very good."

"Of course," Wolfram replied in a passable British accent. He looked to his team. "Did you all hear that, men? We only speak in English from now on."

Krupp handed Wolfram a piece of paper. "I've built a camp in the forest not far from here. The coordinates and a map are there on the paper. It's a good site. I've been in Newfoundland for so long now, so it had to be. There's a cottage there that you can use. Running water is close. I've been hiding there for a little over two months and haven't seen many people."

Wolfram unfolded the paper and studied the hand-drawn map. "Thank you. This is excellent. Did everything go as planned for you?"

"Better. I would say the mission exceeded expectations, and I escaped! I'm sure you heard about the hostel?"

"Yes, everyone has." Wolfram said coldly. "Why did you do it?"

"It was a wonderful target of opportunity," Krupp said with a shrug. "How could I pass on the chance to kill so many of our enemies and strike true fear in their hearts with a single burning match? Now, where's the boat?"

"We have a raft hidden on the beach, that way," Wolfram said while pointing along the beach. "A submarine is waiting offshore."

"And what is your mission?"

"I cannot share that knowledge."

"No matter. I think I know anyway. High Command has wanted to set up a weather station here for some time now. They believe they can get early forecasts on weather patterns if they have a station further west into North America. You see? Not much escapes me."

Wolfram couldn't see it in the darkness, but he believed Krupp was winking at him.

"Before you go, I have to ask … if we can go back to the hostel for a moment, what was it like for you? I mean, once that match was lit?"

Krupp shrugged, "I don't remember much once the fire began. I remember looking back at it while I was running away. I couldn't resist seeing, I suppose. You asked me how I felt. I guess I felt like Lot's wife. How she couldn't resist looking back at the city while it was being destroyed. Did you know that God punished her by turning her into a pillar of salt?" Krupp chuckled. "I hope he doesn't have a similar fate planned for me. When my day comes, I hope it will be less dramatic."

That was as good of a prompt as any for Wolfram to slip a knife into Krupp's right kidney. Krupp drew a sharp breath and struggled. Wolfram's other arm snaked about his prey's neck and held him fast. Wolfram extracted the knife and jammed it into the side of Krupp's neck. A geyser of blood shot skywards. The gurgling told Wolfram he had clipped the windpipe too. Krupp crumpled to the beach rocks. Wolfram cast a glance at his men and saw them watching motionlessly. Surprise was evident on their faces, but discipline held them in place.

Wolfram had completed one goal of the mission. He didn't enjoy killing, but sometimes he wasn't too bothered by it. Killing the operative was one of those times. No matter what Wolfram thought about his enemies, he still respected them as soldiers, and he believed they deserved the chance to fight. They shouldn't be burnt alive like defenceless animals caught in a burning barn. And what about all the innocent civilians who died? Killing them was inexcusable. The fool thought that burning down the hostel would make him a hero. German High Command didn't see it that way. Neither did Wolfram.

He turned to his men. Rank may count for a great deal in the German army, but no officer unexpectedly stabs someone in front of his men and gets away without an explanation.

"Captain, that was not part of the plan," one man said.

"It was one of our mission's objectives to kill this man. Torching that building was the act of a madman, not a soldier. Whether it was ordered or not, Germany was attached to it. This man couldn't be allowed to live long enough to reveal Germany's involvement in the hostel fire. High Command was very clear: When the history of the war is written, this black mark on Germany will not appear."

The soldiers exchanged looks but said nothing. Wolfram shifted his eyes from one face to the next, but he was confident he would receive the answer he expected.

The soldier who had spoken gave Krupp's body a light kick. "What do we do with him?" the soldier said. "Throw him in the sea?"

"No, he'll wash up on the beach again. He's coming with us into the forest. We can hide him there. Now quickly! We need to leave this beach as fast as we can."

Chapter 9

Frank had trouble sleeping that night, so he rose early and occupied himself by cleaning his uniform and then dressing. After putting on his shirt and tie, he slipped his dark blue service jacket over his six-foot frame. On his left arm, he fitted a band that read "R.C.A.F.S.P." He buckled a white belt fitted with ammunition, and his .38 Smith & Wesson revolver hung from his left side. The gun wasn't fancy, but it was reliable. The belt crossed over his right shoulder to give extra support for carrying the equipment's weight. Dark trousers and well-polished shoes finished the lower half of his uniform.

From the hotel, he went directly to the Security Division's office. It was a short walk since the office wasn't located at the constabulary's headquarters on Fort Townshend. Rather, the constabulary kept the division at a building on Water Street.

He arrived at this office and introduced himself to the young secretary. When he asked for directions to the acting sergeant's personal office, she smiled and gestured towards the door directly across from the larger office's main entrance.

He knocked. "Please come in," a voice called from inside.

Upon entering, Frank saw a man sitting on a mahogany desk with his face buried in a document. The nameplate on the door was tarnished and scratched, so Frank was surprised to see that his new partner was so young. The man's thin fingers brushed across the lines of writing, and he moved his lips while he read. At his feet was a pile of dropped envelopes. The sitting man paid no more attention to them than he did to Frank. He had yet to raise his head from the folder. Frank took no offence at that. It gave him the chance to study his new acquaintance.

The man's long nose and smooth features made Frank think of a bird. His delicate, elongated neck didn't do much to change Frank's mind. *If he were an animal, he'd be a goose,* Frank thought.

The man's small frame surprised Frank again. He wasn't very big for a cop. He must have barely met the minimum height requirements. Frank noticed the man's worried expression and how he occasionally shook his head. He either didn't understand the file in front of him or it was causing him anxiety. Frank thought, *Christ, this is the guy I'm supposed to partner with?*

"Hello, I'm Corporal Frank Carousel," he finally said. "I'm glad to finally meet you, Acting Sergeant Fowler."

The man's head popped away from the file, and he jumped down from his seat the way a child would after being caught standing on the furniture.

"Oh, hi there! I'm not him. I was just in here reviewing some of his files. I'm Constable Tobin Aylward."

"Oh, I see."

"Carousel? Now, that's not a Newfoundland name."

"A Newfoundland name?"

"I mean, it isn't a common name here on the island. Where does it come from?"

Frank smiled. "I guess more importantly, where do I come from? I'm with the Royal Canadian Air Force. Listen, do you know where I can find him?"

Tobin stared vacantly, as if he were trying to remember a part of a dream. Frank guessed that he was still thinking about Frank's non-Newfoundland name. He began to think this assignment would be an even greater challenge than he had expected.

Tobin snapped out of his trance and said, "Oh, well, I suppose he'll be back in a minute. I mean, he's got all these files laid out, so I guess he'll be back any second. Oh, there he is now." Tobin pointed behind Frank and towards the larger office's main entrance.

Frank turned around to see a man stepping through the double doors and then crossing the lobby. The distance gave Frank a few seconds to evaluate him.

While Tobin reminded Frank of a goose, Fowler reminded him of a wild boar. He had a broad face and strong build, but he didn't move like he had much flab on him. His thick neck and powerful shoulders strained against his tie and ill-fitting shirt.

Fowler's polished brown leather shoes matched the folded trench coat he carried over his forearm. At the end of that forearm was a striking, gold wristwatch. His hair was overly greased and neatly combed. This was a man who, despite needing his clothes resized, took pride in his appearance.

Before Frank could introduce himself, Fowler shouldered past him. "Out of the way, buddy. You're right in the doorway," he grumbled.

"Oh, excuse me," was all Frank said, though he wanted to say more. He wasn't used to being disregarded, especially when he was in uniform.

Frank knew he would have to make more of an effort. He smiled while Fowler's back was turned to him, and said

"Hello," and extended his hand. "Corporal Frank Carousel. It's nice to meet you, Acting Sergeant Fowler."

Fowler turned, shook his hand, and said, "Just call me 'Jack.' Nice to meet you too," but he still didn't smile. Jack turned to Tobin and said, "What are you doing in my office, Toby?"

"I was just looking over your files for a clue to a related case. I hope you don't mind too much. You had so many files laid out on your desk, so I thought I'd just take a quick peek."

Tobin pointed down at Jack's right hand. Frank's eyes followed. Jack was holding a string of pearls. Frank hadn't noticed that Jack had been holding anything before. He questioned if Jack had been hiding the pearls behind his back, but Frank quickly dismissed the idea. Why would Jack do that?

"A pearl necklace!" Tobin exclaimed. "I'm sure your wife will like a pretty, expensive gift like that, sir."

"You're wrong, Toby. Pearl necklaces aren't expensive. Happy marriages are. And I'll tell you something else while I'm at it. I've never in my life seen a happily married couple who weren't in debt. Besides, what does money matter to you? You got lots of it."

Embarrassment flashed across Tobin's face, which reddened immediately. Tobin left Jack's office without a word. Frank guessed that a similar scene played out every time the young constable interacted with Jack.

Jack took the seat behind his desk, but he didn't invite Frank to sit down. Instead, Jack bent forward to collect the pile of fallen envelopes next to his desk. He grumbled and muttered. Frank didn't catch much of what he said, but he heard a curse and Tobin's name.

Jack finished assembling the mail into a neat stack on the desk and began to read through it. Frank waited for Jack to finish reviewing his mail and again took time to study the man. Jack's pink complexion and small eyes reinforced Frank's opinion that Jack was swinish. It was a mean judgment, and he felt like a jerk for making it. He had to work with Jack, so he would do well to form a higher opinion of him.

Jack finally looked at him. He even smiled. His stained teeth showed that they had seen more than their share of cigarettes and coffee.

"So, you're the one that they told me about," Jack said. "The Canadian sent down to help us through the fire investigation — one that has been officially reported on and concluded, I might add. You know, I don't mean any disrespect, but you're smaller than I thought you'd be. People made such a big deal about you coming to our little island. I suppose I built you up to be something big in my mind."

After he had finished speaking, he continued to look Frank up and down. He even stared at Frank's shoes and snorted, like he saw something about them that he didn't like.

"Do you want to check my hair for lice before we start?" Frank could hear the anger rising in his voice, and he hoped that Jack could hear it too, so he'd know to back off. Then he realized that Jack might be testing him by flicking the jab — trying to get a feel for his new temporary partner. Frank bit his lower lip and said no more.

"It's not often that a foreign nation takes interest in a fire here, but this is a special case, isn't it?"

"And Canada wants to be neighbourly and provide whatever assistance it can with the investigation. Newfoundland may benefit from Canada's expertise."

"Can it now? Don't think that a bunch of islanders could figure it out on their own, eh? You wouldn't have been sent down to our little backwater town just out of neighbourly sentiments. To be quite blunt, I believe that Canada has no faith in Newfoundland to conduct an investigation this important. The stakes are raised once a few dead Canadian army b'ys are thrown into the pot, right, Frank?"

Frank ground his teeth. It was rare that he became annoyed with someone this quickly, but to use Jack's own term, Acting Sergeant Jack Fowler's was a *special case*.

"It seems awfully rushed. The investigation into the fire was wrapped up so fast; it looks like Newfoundland barely cares that it happened at all."

Jack's face darkened. "Don't tell me that people down here don't care, b'y. I was one of the officers who had to ID the bodies. You try having sobbing family members ask you, 'Is it him?' when you can't even tell if the crumbled, charred body is a man or a woman. Yes, you try that on for size, and then come talk to me about what matters."

Frank felt his face grow warm. As with Tobin a moment earlier, he too was now embarrassed in front of Jack.

In a soft voice, Frank said, "I apologize. I overstepped. That was a careless thing to say."

Jack waved his hand to dismiss the matter and said, "It would be very helpful at this point, Frank, if you were to describe your assignment. As you understand, I mean."

"You weren't told already?"

"I want to hear it in your words."

"In a nutshell, I'm supposed to look at the evidence that led up to the constabulary's conclusion and determine if that conclusion makes sense."

"So, your job is to confirm or disconfirm the findings of the investigation based on the evidence already collected. You're not supposed to conduct your own investigation from the ground up. Do you agree?"

"I agree that's what my assignment is. Though, I think it would be best if I did perform my own original investigation. What if the constabulary missed something while collecting evidence?"

"Can we agree that your authority is very limited here? You're essentially a guest working with the Newfoundland Constabulary. Furthermore, the Newfoundland Constabulary has fully already conducted its own investigation with full authority."

"Full authority? What about the fire department?"

Jack waved his hand again — a gesture that Frank was beginning to hate. "The city's fire department is a part of the Newfoundland Constabulary," Jack said. "So, between the fire department and the Security Division of the constabulary, the whole investigation was undertaken and overseen by us."

"And now maybe it's a good time for you to tell me where you come into the picture."

"I'm supposed to be your handler over the next week or so. Make sure you get the police records you need, toss you a map of the city, show you where city hall is, maybe connect you to the right people — stuff of that sort. Anything else you need while you are here, just let me know. Here's the case folder." Jack pushed a brown folder across his desk with a flick of his thick fingers. The gentle push on the overpacked folder sent some of its contents sliding out. Frank noticed that there weren't any other case folders, thick or thin, sitting on Fowler's desk and concluded that this hostel fire was still consuming a lot of Jack's time.

"So, we're partners?"

"Yeah. I suppose we're *temporary* partners, if you want to think of it that way. Jack rubbed the deep lines in his forehead and closed his eyes. The man probably hadn't relaxed since the war started. The hostel case had probably drained whatever he still had in his fuel tank.

"I was thinking I'd take you to the hostel this morning as soon as we finish up here," Jack said.

"Will you and I be working alone on this?"

"I wish. We'll have to put up with Constable Tobin Aylward. That's the moron who just left my office. He never should have made it into the police. He doesn't have the size or the brains for it. But Toby's father's got money, and he got him into the constabulary. If you want a good government job on this island, it helps if your family already works in the public service, or if you come from money." Jack huffed and added, "That's true anyplace, I suppose."

"If he's so bad, then why are we burdened with him?"

"To be honest, I think it's to punish me. Don't worry, I'll do everything I can to keep that village idiot out of our hair. There is one thing that I'm curious about, Frank."

"Go ahead."

Jack leaned forward, over his desk, and he was close enough that Frank could smell his breath — coffee and old meat filled Frank's nose.

"If your duty is to review a fire case and its conclusion, then why were you assigned in the first place? Why not send a fire marshal or someone like that?"

"I've received specialty training in sabotage investigation."

"So, Canada's air force thinks it was sabotage?"

"Haven't you considered it, sir?"

Jack waved his hand dismissively. "Back to you, though. There's lots of people in Canada's military who have been trained same as you, so there must be some other reason *you* got this assignment. Come on, Frank, who'd you piss off to get this job?"

"My brother was one of the soldiers killed in the fire. I volunteered for this."

Jack didn't raise an eyebrow or give much other indication that he was shocked at the news. He was trying to remain stone-faced. Regardless, Frank could see a small scratch of sympathy — too small to describe in detail — on that boiled boot Jack Fowler called a face.

"I'm sorry," Jack said coolly. "I remember, now that you mention it, there was a victim identified with the last name *Carousel*. I'm sure he was a hell of a military man."

"He was." Frank reached for his cigarette pack from his coat pocket — his way of breaking from an uncomfortable conversation. "So, what about the public and the newspapers? What do they think happened?"

"Just as you'd expect: Some say it was an accident — albeit, a huge one bound to leave a nasty scar on the city's history. Some say it was an act of war. Everyone says it was a tragedy."

"And is that why the city put in place a curfew the day after the fire? Because it was an accident?"

Jack's grim expression told Frank that he was aggravating his new acquaintance. Frank admitted to himself that he was being a little smart-mouthed.

"And what do you believe the truth is, Jack? I mean, between us *partners*."

Jack inhaled deeply and blew the smoke out of his nose. Frank thought he would have to repeat the question. Jack finally spoke, "It was no coincidence, sir, that a building filled with Allied servicemen went up in flames during wartime. It wasn't an accident, or faulty wiring, or God's hand, or anything else other than a planned mass murder. That's right — a murder. To hell with any notion of sabotage. If it were deliberate, then it wouldn't be sabotage. Sabotage is when you attack an inanimate thing, like a bridge or a railway. If this fire was deliberate, then it was an attack on *people*. It just happened to be done by setting fire to the building they were in at the time. That's murder in my book."

Frank smiled at that. Now he was getting somewhere with this asshole. "Well, Jack, it's nice to see that there's something we agree on."

***

The new partners spent the next half hour getting to know each other better over coffee. Jack had even offered Frank a seat in his office, which Frank took as a sign that his new-found partner was warming up to him. They both talked about where they grew up. Jack said he was from some distant fishing village along Newfoundland's coast. Frank couldn't manage to pronounce the name of it, but he wasn't sure if that was because it was a French name, or because he was having a hard time with Jack's accent. Likewise, Frank told Jack about his hometown, Dundas, Ontario, but he could tell the name was equally unimportant to Jack. After finishing their cups, they headed out to visit the remains of the hostel.

"If it's all the same, why don't we walk there instead of driving? It'll be a good way for me to become familiar with the city."

"I never planned on driving to begin with. The hostel was only on Duckworth Street, the next street over. It'll only take us a few minutes to get there."

Jack put on his grey wool coat that hung to his knees. "I never knew that you planned on staying here for so long that you would want to get to know the place, but it's all right with me."

Frank noticed the sound of church bells as they left the building. They sounded as if they might be coming from the cathedral he had passed the night before. He wasn't surprised to hear the bells clanging on a weekday. "The war keeps the bells ringing every day of the week now. It's the same back in Canada."

Jack nodded. "Yeah, no shortage of funerals these days. When this war is over, I never want to hear another church bell again," he said.

When driving through the city, the downtown's narrow streets had felt crammed. Now that Frank was walking, they felt cozy. There was an intimacy here he would expect to find in a hamlet, not in a modern capital city. And he liked that St. John's had an aged feel about it. *Like how it feels when you climb a deep-rooted tree or sit on an antique church pew*, he thought. It felt like a place where traditions matter, ritual is embraced, and history is kept alive. Here, history wasn't something remote that had ceased to exist. It was breathed by everyone every day as much as the salty sea air that now filled Frank's lungs.

Frank once again studied the rows of rainbow houses in their purples, reds, and oranges. In the daylight, their full vibrancy could be seen. There was something playful about them. Frank liked that. It added to the city's charm.

"We'll be there soon. The fire happened only a stone's throw away from the office," Jack said. "So, what do you do in Canada? Chase after spies for the air force? Things like that?"

"Not so much spies. When the war broke out, Canada rounded up so many of the Nazi sympathizers and fascists that it almost completely wiped out Germany's chances for espionage in Canada. I suppose there's no worries of Nazi sympathizers and European-style fascism in Newfoundland. I doubt if that stuff really took hold here. From what I can tell, there doesn't seem to be much of a difference between all the people living here — white, British backgrounds. It doesn't really seem to be the sort of place where different or new ideas catch on."

The moment it left his mouth, Frank realized what he had just said. Jack snorted, making no effort to hide his disapproval. This may well have been the worst goddamn first meeting of Frank's life. Frank tried to apologize, but Jack cut him off, "You'd be surprised what catches on here, b'y, as well as what ideas outsiders are bringing here these days. This city is a hotbed for intelligence, my good man. The FBI, British Security Service, Mounties — you name the organization, they're operating here. We work with all intelligence sections."

A pack of Girl Guides ran past them. Their arms were full of Hershey bars and Cokes. There wasn't enough room for everyone on the sidewalk, so the two men sidestepped to give way to the girls.

"You see those girls with all those treats in their hands? I tell you, the children here didn't have all of that a few years ago. The good thing is that the war effort's poured a great deal of money into the country. There's plenty of construction and maintenance jobs at the new bases. Many American servicemen spending that fat Yankee dollar helps too. It's a job to find a seat in a bar or restaurant these days. Many store owners have seen their profits double in just the last two years!"

Frank believed it. From the crowded cafés, restaurants, and lunch counters he could see, it was hard to reach any conclusion other than that the war meant big business for the city.

An American Jeep with a large white star painted on its front splashed them as it passed. The Jeep came to a halt, and the driver yelled in a thick New England accent, "Sorry about that, boys! Can I give you a ride anywhere?"

"No thanks, b'y. We're fine."

The soldier gave them a wave and sped off, perhaps a little too fast for the city's potholed roads. No sooner than he had left them, an American army truck sped past and splashed them again.

"Dammit!" Frank yelled. He wiped some muddy water off his face.

Jack winked at him. "To be sure, there's been a great deal of benefits that have come with the Friendly Invasion. There's lots more jobs and imports from America. But at the other end of that see-saw, you have crowding, too much traffic, higher costs for everything, and a hell of a lot of what I call *street thuggery*. I guess we need to take all the bad with the good, right?"

"There are so many Americans here! My God, where do they all stay?"

Jack chuckled. "Oh, they stay here and there. Some stay in bases and camps that have been built around the town. Some sleep on board the ships that brought them here."

"And some stay in hostels that have been set up just for them. Like the one that burnt down."

"Yeah, just like that one. Or like this one here." Jack pointed to a new YMCA. American country music trickled through its open window. Someone inside was keeping rhythm on a guitar. He strummed along as well as any performer Frank had heard on a stage. Frank wished he had time to go inside to listen longer.

If only Tom had stayed in that one instead. He knew that in the end his brother's death came down to luck. Frank wondered if the men staying inside the Y — the lucky ones — knew it too.

Chapter 10

The two men passed a large brick building, and Frank finally saw it — not the remains of the hostel, but the city's harbour. He had been so engrossed by the streetscape and conversation that he hadn't yet looked towards the waterfront. He was now standing only yards away from it. He breathed deeply, and his eyes widened at the spectacle.

The harbour was crammed with naval ships. None were large compared to the colossal battleships, but there were so many. The vessels were moored bow to stern, forming a shipscape that couldn't be fully surveyed with one straight view. Frank had to pan across the harbour's expanse to see it all.

A crew of sailors hustled their sea-chests up a gangway of a minesweeper. The ship's officer bawled at them to step lively. Next to that vessel was a Canadian destroyer. The vessel looked like one of the outdated destroyers, which Frank had read was given to Britain by America a couple of years earlier. They were a generation behind the best of the American and British ships. Frank wondered how well that rustbucket before him could keep pace with its allies on the high seas.

A crane lifted a small boat onto the deck of the destroyer while a ship's deckhand yelled at the crane operator with all the fury of the neighbouring ship's first mate. Watching the two curse and complain, in parallel, only fifty feet apart, made him chuckle. When Jack saw, he joined in the laughter. "Good thing those two aren't serving on the same ship. Don't know if there would be room for both of them!"

Frank's smile grew — the two of them were starting to get along.

Frank saw a small warship and was able to identify it as a Flower-class corvette from what he'd seen in the newspapers. He looked at the corvette's lone four-inch gun and wondered what good it would do in a fight against most warships. He examined the ship from bow to stern and guessed it couldn't be much more than two hundred feet long — a rowboat compared to the giant battleships of the American and British fleets. He knew smaller vessels were fine for coastal operations, but in deep ocean, the large waves tossed them like flowers in a thunderstorm. Shivering and wet crews couldn't sleep, and they exhausted themselves just trying to keep their balance while doing their jobs. Frank had heard that if you served in the Canadian navy, the worst place to get assigned was on a Flower-class corvette.

Jack followed Frank's gaze and said, "I know what you're thinking. Thank God we aren't on one of those corvettes, right? I've heard lots of stories about those things. Too slow, too shaky, and too damn uncomfortable."

"I've heard worse than that. When a corvette sinks, the depth charges it has on board go underwater, and they've already been set to blow at certain depths. So a lot of sailors who go into the water alive still get blown to pieces by their own bombs."

"Yeah, I've heard that too."

"Jesus, do you think it's true?"

Jack grimaced and snorted. "If it's just a rumour, then it's a widespread one that has been going around for a long time. In my experience, well-travelled rumours that persist have some truth to them."

Jack lit a smoke with one flick of his lighter. He took a short inhale, blew out the smoke, and said, "Pay attention, and I'll teach you how it works now," Jack said. "You see all those warships? It's called the Newfoundland Escort Force." The pride in his voice was unmistakable.

"Escort service?" Frank asked.

"Convoys of ships, sometimes fifty or sixty of them, are formed over in Nova Scotia in places like Halifax. They sail for Europe with some naval escorts to protect them from submarine attacks. These aren't the big gun battleships, mind you. These are just little corvettes and destroyers, mostly. Not all these smaller warships are well-suited for transatlantic travel. They roll a lot in the deep ocean's big waves; they don't hold enough fuel — that sort of thing. It's almost as hard on the crews as it is on the ships. Trust me, I've been down here when one of those tiny corvettes pulls into port after they've been out in bad storm. I've seen their masts cracked and their canvases ripped. And the poor men are so wet, sick, and exhausted. They look like they could sleep for a week!"

"But when the wolf packs attack, they fight, right?"

"Oh yes, they put up a fight, but the scorecard usually ends in the Germans' favour. For now, anyway." Frank took a long draw from his cigarette and threw it towards the harbour, but a gust of wind carried it away before it could reach the water.

"Anyhow, where was I? Oh, yes. So, convoys only get escorted part of the way across the ocean by those vessels. The convoys meet up with another group of escorts, fresh

ones, off the coast of Newfoundland. They escort the
merchant ships most of the way over to Europe. St. John's is
where the first batch of these escort vessels put in to refuel,
rest, and do some repairs.

"Once the convoys get close to Europe, a new batch of
escorts meets up with them out in the ocean, and the escort
vessels that came out of Newfoundland then head over to
Iceland to replenish themselves. Later, they pick up
westbound convoys."

"And do the whole process again, but in reverse!"

"You got it. See, b'y, I knew I could teach you something."

"So essentially the role of the warships is to be like a sort
of sheepdog navy that protects cargo — material and human
— from the German wolf packs."

"That's a good way of looking at it. A bunch of metal
sheepdogs!" Jack guffawed.

Frank studied the flags and names of each ship. He noted
the many nations represented and pointed out a few flags.
"The Americans, the British, the Canadians — they're all
here, aren't they?" he said.

"Oh yes, they're all here. St. John's isn't a seaport
anymore. It's a goddamn base," Jack said. "It looks like they
have every navy vessel in the world stuck on this little patch
of water. Sure, take a good look at all those ships sitting in
the middle of the harbour. Along the waterfront, ships don't
even have anywhere to tie on, so some need to drop anchor
out there in the middle."

Frank saw a cluster of four corvettes lashed together side
by side out in the middle of the harbour. Their decks were
so close that a sailor could walk from his own vessel to visit
a friend on another, eat on a third, and deliver a message to
a fourth, with his feet being his only means of travel.

"So, how do the guys get to shore when they want to get off the ships?" Frank asked.

"Some of the local fishermen use their small fishing boats to ferry sailors from their ships to the docks. But they need to pay a fare for the service."

"So that's another way the locals are making the most out of servicemen being in town."

"Yeah, it's not a bad way to earn some extra money."

"Are all these warships assigned to mid-ocean escort?"

"Well, like I said, that job's more likely given to the corvettes and destroyers." Jack pointed to a pair of vessels to their right. "See those over there? Those are armed yachts. Private vessels bought or commandeered by the navies, outfitted with some weapons and gear, and then put into service. They're more likely to be used for work in shallow waters. Good for coastal patrols and guarding harbours. They get used a lot for training crews too."

Frank studied the yachts. Both of the big vessels still had a civilian look. There were hardly any guns on them.

How strange it was that the navy had purchased private vessels and outfitted them for war. But, he supposed, every navy had to make do with what they could find.

Frank gasped when he saw a tugboat pulling a demolished ship towards the dockyard. The victim had a colossal, semicircular hole that ran clean through the ship's bow. Either a giant shark had taken a forty-foot bite out of it, or the ship was the victim of a torpedo. That the ship had kept afloat was a credit to its crew. Frank crouched to get a better look at the damage and was surprised that he could see such a large section of the harbour's opposite side.

As if that wasn't wonder enough, a fishing boat then used the hole as a short-cut. The little rowboat crossed from the ship's port side to starboard without having to manoeuvre around the ship's bow or stern. The rowing fisherman saw Frank staring at him and gave a smile and a wink, as if to say, "I do this a dozen times a day!"

Jack chuckled. "That's something, isn't it? How boats just cut through each other like that?"

"You've seen them do that before?"

"Many times," Jack said. His tone turned grim. "I suppose I've seen it too often."

Frank expected the waterfront to be active, but this was something else. Not all the activity was military, either. Civilian life needed to continue, in spite of the war. Fishermen sorted their catch on the dock while stevedores stepped around coils of rigging. Men busied themselves packing goods at the warehouses. Some sailors hurriedly unloaded a coal ship. Nervous cattle bellowed while being off-loaded from another vessel. The poor beasts, frightened by the commotion of the docks, looked ready to jump into the harbour and flee.

There were schooners that looked like they had just sailed in from the last century. Their masts stood like crucifixes across the harbour. Their sails flapped in the city's perpetual breeze.

Frank recalled the map he had studied the previous night. He remembered the harbour's sock shape and got his bearings. He was somewhere in the middle of the harbour's north side. From his position, he had a wide view of the harbour. It was smaller than it had appeared on the map, and it snuggled deep into the surrounding hills.

He stared across the harbour at the south side. *Sparse*, he thought. He saw forested hills with nothing on them of note — just a few homes. He saw several fishing docks that he was certain were made of wood and a couple of sturdier ones that were surfaced in some sort of masonry. What kind, he couldn't tell, but he assumed it was concrete, like the dock on the north side.

To Frank, what was most interesting about the south side wasn't what was there but what was absent. There was very little infrastructure in place. Whereas the north side was full of cranes, buildings, motor pools, and people hustling to complete the day's work, the south side was underdeveloped. Frank saw only a couple of ships, which were barely large enough to be worthy of the title.

The south side's lack of detail hinted at incompleteness. It was as if an artist had painted the rest of the harbour and lost interest in the south side. Frank wondered why the south side had not developed on the same path and thought the low hills overshadowing its docks could be the answer. Perhaps the terrain proved too difficult for construction.

He looked to the harbour's entrance and watched a whaling ship just passing through. The vessel has been modernized since the days of Herman Melville, but it still made Frank think of *Moby-Dick*. He chuckled. Perhaps a modern-day Ishmael or Starbuck was within the ship's metal hull, checking the engines or boiler.

"My God, the opening is so small." Frank said. "Can you even see the city from out there in the ocean?"

"Not so well. You really need to sail into the Narrows before the city sort of opens up to you and you can see all the buildings. But I suppose that's why we call the opening the *Narrows* in the first place."

Frank squinted to get a better look at the entrance's finer details. Then he remembered he had brought his binoculars. He removed them from his leather case. After adjusting their focus, he could see the tip of the Narrows, just barely kissing the wider Atlantic that lay beyond. A lighthouse lay there, along with a set of buildings he surmised were for harbour protection.

"What's all of that?" he said and pointed to them.

"Oh, that's Fort Amherst, where they have the examination battery. There's a load of firepower there, ready to cut apart any suspicious ship that doesn't pass the test!"

Frank panned the harbour's side and saw that Fort Amherst wasn't the only firing position. More gun sites ringed the harbour's entrance.

"God help any Nazi foolish enough to come through the Narrows, eh Jack?"

"Let me tell you, that harbour's impenetrable! It's got anti-submarine netting, the gun batteries. There's even a little field of sea mines placed just outside the Narrows."

Frank looked to his left, the northeast part of the harbour, at a hill that loomed over the Narrows — grey, bare rock, with sporadic patches of moss and other low-lying vegetation. Capping the hill was a stone structure, shaped like a rook from a chess set. It was small, but with no other structures on the hilltop, it looked formidable.

"What's that little castle up there?" Frank said and pointed.

"Oh, that's Cabot Tower, and the hill it's on is called Signal Hill. It's a local attraction." Fowler said. "If we have time for sightseeing, I'll take you up there."

Frank looked at the base of the hill and saw it was belted with a line of buildings. At first he thought it was a shantytown of roughly made structures. On closer inspection, he saw it was more akin to an old-fashioned maritime village.

High wharves, with small fishing sheds attached, stood on rickety, slanted posts that crossed each other at tight angles. The fishing flakes, on which men would lay out their salted fish to dry in the warmer months, were strewn across in no apparent order. To Frank, the assembly looked like a house of cards that might fall over, sending the whole bizarre mosaic tumbling into the sea. Frank had never seen anything like it before. He was certain that one day a small landslide would push the clutter of buildings into the ocean.

These work spaces were backed by wooden houses with sagging roofs. He saw a narrow road that traced the coastline, separating all the pastel houses from the wharves and fishing sheds. He guessed this split was one of the few divisions between work and family life in the little village.

He saw at least two dozen fishing boats over there, all the same small, open variety. All the vessels he saw had sails and oars. Frank saw none with outboard engines. As well, none of the boats looked more than twenty feet long. Some had already been pulled out of the water and were lying next to the wharves and storehouses or sitting on small slipways.

Like the rest of Signal Hill, the village was treeless. The rocky slopes had only green patches of moss and short grass. He took particular notice of the crooked line of telephone poles that snaked throughout the village. The poles not only carried signals, they were signals — symbols of modernity.

"That's The Battery, that bunch of houses and stuff over there." Jack said.

"The Battery? It looks like a — I don't know what you would call it. Some sort of little hamlet inside the city?"

"I guess so. I can take you over there. There isn't much to see but some wharves and a few fishing boats. I suppose there's the new supply dock that the US Army put up. That thing is over six hundred feet long! That's probably the newest thing built over there in the last fifty years! Got the best cranes you could care for, a huge warehouse."

Frank could make out the dock. It was the only one of its kind over there that came close to approaching Jack's description. "I'll pass, thanks," Frank said. He doubted that a supply dock was anything worth visiting.

Jack waved his other arm across the harbour. He did it slowly, as if to emphasize its expanse. "As for this harbour, they had to put in a lot of work on it to make it half serviceable for the navies," Jack said. "You should have seen it a couple of years ago before they built the new warehouses, the repair shops, the smithies, and the new docks. They had to dredge the hell out of it too. After five hundred years of dumping rubbish into it, the harbour's bottom built up. They had to dig up all the filth out of her like it was a big tub of spoiled lard."

Frank surveyed the waterfront from end to end. It wasn't difficult to tell which parts were newly constructed — their concrete had few cracks, their metal was rustless. Meanwhile, the older sections of the harbour were almost completely made of wood, much of it aged and in need of a good paint job.

Jack lifted his chin slightly and straightened his posture. "So, what do you think of it all, b'y?" he said.

Frank smiled when he again saw how proud Jack was of the harbour and the magnitude of its work. There was only one proper response to Jack's question.

"I'm amazed! St. John's is turning out to be so much more than I expected," he said. Hearing his own words, Frank realized that he wasn't only pandering to Jack. He meant what he had said with all sincerity. St. John's truly had surprised him.

"Oh, yeah? How so?"

"Just … more. More of everything. This place has more spark to it than I first thought it had."

Jack grinned and patted Frank on the shoulder. "Sometime maybe I'll show you the nightlife!"

A rumble came from above. Frank thought it was another air patrol passing overhead, but then he recognized the sound as thunder.

His shoulders tightened. Thunder's deep crackle had a way of flooding him not with fear, exactly, but with apprehension. He looked at Jack and saw that he felt it too.

"Bloody weather," Jack said. "We better hurry up. The rain will be down on us soon. Oh well, at least there's no snow down. That's a lucky thing, it being November and all." Jack lit a cigarette. He pulled his coat tight over his broad shoulders and had difficulty fastening the buttons. "Yeah, this goddamn rain. We got plenty of it now, b'y, but where was it all on the night of the fire? You know, when we needed it?"

Jack pointed to the remains of the hostel ahead of them. Its charred beams had been soaked by the many downpours since the fire. Despite the rain, the ground was still layered in feet of ash and debris. The sidewalk in front of the hostel was covered in a thick layer of soot that had turned to black sludge. Not even the city's constant rain could seem to wash it away.

Some metal beams stood as quiet reminders that the hostel's remains had once been something more than a heap of ash. How anyone could make sense of the mess, Frank couldn't tell. A boxy brick structure stood in the middle of that heap. Frank supposed it to be all that was left of the fireplace and chimney. He could make out blackened water pipes running through the length of the ruins.

He also noticed that some of the neighbouring buildings had scorch marks and realized how close the city had come to losing its entire downtown. And what did this place now mean to the city? The locals probably viewed it as hallowed ground. The hairs on the back of Frank's neck raised.

He compared the ruins to the photograph he had studied the night before at his hotel — the one that showed the hostel's sign, its double doors, and those American soldiers frozen in time, eternally laughing and goofing off next to the truck. This was where his brother died.

"They say that most of the people who perished died from smoke inhalation, not burning, or anything like that," Jack said softly. "It was fast for them and it never hurt."

"Thanks, Jack." Frank said without looking at him. He believed that they died from smoke inhalation, but he knew that the rest — about it being quick and painless — was bullshit. He appreciated what Jack was trying to do for him.

"Did you want to go inside and take a look?" Jack asked.

"Inside what? It doesn't have a roof or any walls," Frank said. Still, he took Jack's meaning and stepped into the blackened skeleton.

He studied the floor's scorched boards and gaping holes. An unlucky step would send him into the basement. He looked for a firm spot to place his foot, and then Jack's hand fell on his shoulder.

"Don't just step anywhere," Jack said. "Step where I step. I've been here before, so I know the safe places."

Jack made a few large steps across the floor. His cigarette dangled between his lips while he waved his arms for balance. Frank was surprised at the big man's nimbleness.

He felt much more confident about his chances. If a brick like Jack could cross the floor safely, then what did Frank have to fear?

He strode across the floor, stepping where Jack had stepped. He anchored himself against the remains of a beam and began studying the wreckage for any obvious clues.

"I suppose it's good to come here. To get a feel for the place and all. But after the site has been picked over by other investigators and the rain has had weeks to wash away evidence, I doubt that I'll find much."

"So, what do you look for when you examine a scene like this?" Jack asked.

Frank shrugged. "You look for any lessons the ashes can teach you. You look for clues about what types of incendiaries were used, the ignition device used, things like that." Frank didn't want to give a detailed answer. He suspected that Jack was only testing his knowledge. Jack looked to be in his early forties, and Frank assumed he'd probably had at least twenty years of experience as a policeman, so he would already know what fire investigators look for.

"Before you ask, the answer is 'no.' This isn't my first time examining a burnt down building," Frank added. And that was true — it was his *fourth* time. But none of the three other buildings were as big as the hostel, nor did any of those fires involve loss of life. He wasn't about to tell Jack that, though.

Frank felt drops of rain on the back of his neck. Again, the thunder growled above him. Soon those few drops would be a tempest. He didn't have much time left on site.

"Hi, how's the work going?" A woman's voice sounded behind them, interrupting the tour.

The two men turned. Frank noticed a rust-coloured dress fit neatly over a slim figure. It complemented the woman's auburn hair and contrasted with her clear, ivory skin. Her right arm was in a sling, and her left hand held a brown paper bag. Frank glanced appreciatively at her legs but quickly looked away, hoping no one had caught him.

The woman flashed them a brilliant smile and pulled a brown wallet out of the bag. "I've got your badge and wallet. You left them at the house this morning. I figured you would need your identification," she said.

Embarrassment crossed Jack's face as he took the badge and wallet. "Jesus, what kind of cop leaves his badge at home? Thanks, I don't know what I would do sometimes without you, girly. Frank, may I introduce Beth? Beth, this is Corporal Frank Carousel. He's with the Canadian air force's military police. He and I will be working together on the fire case."

Beth smiled and extended her left hand. Frank took it and thought that it matched her face — smooth and cool.

"It's a pleasure to make your acquaintance," he said.

"Likewise. I'm sorry to interrupt, but there isn't a day that goes by that Jack doesn't leave something back at the place — his hat, his gloves, his wallet, his house key. You name it." She giggled. She had a beautiful laugh and a nice smile to go with it.

"Well, he's a lucky man to have a wife who would run over his badge and wallet to him."

"Oh, she's not my wife." Jack said. "Beth's my little sister."

"Oh, I thought you were married!" Frank said. He then noticed the absence of a wedding band on Beth's ring finger. Things were looking up!

"Are you having any luck, Corporal Carousel?" she asked.

"With the investigation? I just arrived here a moment ago, and I'm guessing that the weather isn't going to let me stay here for much longer." Frank held out his hand, palm up to show the rain. "Maybe we shouldn't have spent so much time admiring the harbour, hey Jack?"

"Oh, you saw all the ships, then?" she asked.

"Yes, I got a good look at how packed it is. Jack told me they're on escort duty?"

"Most of them, yes. Some of those convoys get to be over fifty ships in size, you know?"

Frank raised his eyebrows and pretended that Jack hadn't told him the same thing less than thirty minutes ago. "I hadn't realized that the operations were that big. Well, anyway, those were some fine-looking ships that I saw down there." He had misgivings about some of the vessels he had seen, but he wasn't about to tell her. Frank believed that in these chaotic times, men had an obligation to keep women's spirits up.

Jack cursed as he wiped the freshly fallen rain from his greasy hair.

"Jack, watch your mouth!" Beth said.

"Sorry, but this rain's always got to ruin everything, don't it? Well, we've had a busy morning. Let's have lunch. We can always come back here another time, if you don't find enough details in those files I gave you."

"You're right," Frank said. "I'm sure those files will answer a lot of my questions."

"Would you like to come over to our place for tea, Corporal?" Beth asked.

Frank was surprised by the invitation, and Jack clearly was as well. "I would love to have tea with you, but I don't know how your brother would feel about me going over to your place."

"It's *my* house. Beth lives with me," Jack said. "And it's only tea, for Christ's sake. Come on, it isn't too far from here. Beth here will fix you something to eat!"

Chapter 11

Beth had always been shy around men, especially handsome ones. Her big brother's presence only magnified the awkwardness.

Still, on the walk home she tried to push that from her mind and sneak a better look at Jack's *ringless* colleague. As she was admiring his height and beautiful eyes, she noticed that Frank didn't seem phased by Jack at all. Most men were intimidated by her brother, even if they wouldn't admit it, but Frank brushed off Jack's crudeness like a man who had been handling guys like her older brother all his life. It was this confidence that really drew Beth in. Nonetheless, having Jack around made her uncomfortable, and to make matters worse, bolts of pain drove up her back. She had her painkillers with her, but she didn't want to take them in front of Frank.

A strong breeze blew through her dress. Why, for goodness' sake, did she decide to wear such a thin dress in November? She trembled but didn't complain. She wanted Frank to like her, and she believed men didn't like women who griped. So she walked on the inside of the sidewalk close to the houses and storefronts and used Frank and Jack as a windbreak.

The trio moved down Aldershot Street towards Jack's place. It wasn't too far from the hostel. They only had to walk up a hill from the downtown, and then Jack's place was part of the way down that hill's opposite slope.

Jack explained to Frank, "You see, this neighbourhood of St. John's really started getting built up after the Great War. A lot of servicemen came home and put themselves here. The city changed some of the street names to match with the places where our regiment served. Cairo Street, Malta Street, Suez Street. This street we're on now, my street, was once called Plum Street. But they changed the name to Aldershot Street because the regiment was stationed in Aldershot, England, at one point."

Beth tried to read Frank's face to see if he was interested in what her brother was saying. If so, she would try to wedge in a little of her own knowledge about the neighbourhood. But Frank only raised his eyebrows and gave a slight nod. Beth decided it wasn't the time to cut in.

"Speaking of houses, Beth, I saw a house for rent down on Gower Street," Jack said. "Nice place. Right near your work."

"What colour is it?"

"Affordable. The name of the colour is *affordable*. Any more questions, girly?"

Beth's face flushed. It's wasn't bad enough that she had to live with him like a charity case? Now he was picking out a home for her and calling her *girly* in front of a man — a tall man, a tall, attractive man with deep blue eyes that reminded Beth of the ocean in summertime.

They arrived at Jack's house. It was the same style as its many row house neighbours. It even had the same sort of garish colours — canary yellow with a sapphire blue door. Beth was worried what Frank would think when he saw it. She was relieved when he smiled.

"I hope the house isn't too foolish for you, Frank."

"Jesus, Beth!" Jack said. "You're talking like you're the one who owns the place, instead of someone who just sleeps in the den."

Beth felt blood rush to her cheeks. She hoped Frank wouldn't see her blush. She hated it when her brother said such embarrassing things so casually. Why did he have to do that?

They went inside. Beth cast her eyes across the kitchen to check that it was clean. Thankfully her brother had placed his breakfast dishes in the sink instead of leaving them on the table.

The phone was already ringing when they entered. Jack dashed to the parlour to answer it. Beth began taking the leftovers out of the refrigerator. Frank stepped to her side and said, "Here, let me help you with that," and he began loading cold roast beef onto a plate.

"That's all right. I know I only have one good arm now, but I can still manage to take up a few plates of supper," Beth said.

While she was putting lunch together, she again wondered about Frank's impression of the home. The place didn't speak of wealth, but Jack always did pride himself on living humbly. Beth had never pointed out the contradiction to him.

The kitchen's pine furniture and decorations were equally plain. A painting of Christ feeding the masses with a loaf of bread hung over the table. A leafy, green plant that Beth couldn't name sat on top of a cabinet. Its vines tumbled down the cabinet's side. Next to it hung a crucifix. Beth wondered if Frank was noticing any of this. *Of course he is*, she thought, *he wouldn't be much of a cop if he didn't.*

Beth gestured for Frank to sit at the table and help himself to some of the biscuits lying on a plate at the table's centre. Frank accepted the offer and pointed to a pile of letters lying on the table. The addresses varied, but they were all places in Europe and they all had the same sender — Billy Fowler.

"It's important that you write a lot to servicemen. There's many of them posted at my base back home, and there's nothing more heartbreaking than a serviceman's disappointment when the mail arrives and there isn't a single letter or a care package for him. You have a family member over there, eh?"

"My nephew. Jack's son." Beth said. She stopped preparing the food and straightened her suffering back as much as it would let her. "You ought to know this before you say anything to Jack: Billy was killed in action two months ago."

She could feel the room getting colder. Frank's face dropped.

She continued, "He was on a British destroyer that got torpedoed off the coast of France. All hands lost. We don't even have a body to put in the ground."

"I'm so sorry," Frank said.

Beth nodded her thanks and turned back to the leftovers. All that was missing from this conversation was Frank asking about her paralyzed arm, or her jabbering on about her separation from Gerald. God, she never wanted to have to explain that arsehole. She hadn't wanted her brother around earlier, but now she couldn't wait for him to return from the parlour.

"So, what about Mrs. Fowler?" Frank asked. "Where is she today?"

"She's gone now. Staying with her people for a time."

"Visiting a relative, eh?"

Beth hesitated. Her sister-in-law's absence from the house was another issue, and it wasn't her place to explain it. But she couldn't leave Frank's question unanswered.

"Jack and his wife, Ellie, are having some difficulties at this time. All marriages do."

Frank looked embarrassed. She was certain he regretted asking.

"Poor guy. I can't imagine what that would be like," was all that he said.

"To be sure. It's hard enough being a police officer in this city these days. It makes a big difference if a policeman has a wife to stand behind him. Jack doesn't have that anymore. Maybe he'll never have it again." She wanted to kick herself in the rear. Why did she have to be so gloomy? Men hated gloomy women.

Frank wriggled in his seat. "So, you live here with your brother, eh?" Just the two of you?"

"I don't have a man or any children with me, if that's what you're getting at. I mean—."

"You don't have to explain. Maybe I've asked enough questions for my first visit here."

"No, I know it must look odd for a woman my age to be single and living in her brother's house. I—."

Jack entered the kitchen and spoke loudly enough to cut her off. "Frank, I just got off the phone with one of the guys at the station. He called about the fire. Come over into the parlour and we can talk about it better in there. Bring your case and files with you, too."

Once the two men left, Beth hastily collected the letters on the table. She stuffed them into a kitchen drawer. Jack wouldn't like it if they were left lying around, even if he had been the one who left them there.

The kettle whistled, and Beth took it from the stove. What a fool she was. Has it been so long since I've talked to a man that I've forgotten how to do it altogether?

She hissed and rubbed her twisting back. It was time for those painkillers.

***

She and Gerald had been enjoying a Sunday drive around the bay. She was admiring the shoreline while the car scooted through the coastal roads.

"These roads are enough to test any man's driving," Gerald used to say. He was right. Plenty of sharp turns and blind hills.

It was while they were cresting one of those hills that a truck popped up in front of them. Gerald didn't have time to swerve.

Both vehicles were destroyed, but everyone lived. Gerald and the other man recovered from their wounds in only weeks; Beth's lingered for months. Sensation slowly returned to her right arm, but the doctor said that some of the nerve damage may be permanent. He recommended she rest, get some light exercise now and then, and take a basket of painkillers to treat her back.

The accident frayed their marriage. Her injuries — and the complications attendant to them — eroded Gerald's spirit. Taking care of her while minding the shop by himself was exhausting him. He became emotionally distant. When they should have been making the most of their time together, Gerald was detached and living in his own head. She would sometimes ask him what he was thinking, and he would shake his head as if he had been disturbed and say he was thinking of nothing at all.

The lack of physical intimacy didn't help. Neither of them had expected sex to begin right after the accident, but both thought it would gradually resume. It didn't. He took to sleeping on the chesterfield. Beth would have preferred that he sleep in another house altogether than know that he was out there sleeping in their living room while she failed to fill the lonely bed every night.

Regrettably, she got her wish. That was around the time Gerald began tomcatting around two local pubs. The sort of places that real ladies avoided. The sort of places where it wasn't frowned upon for women to enjoy themselves unaccompanied by men.

More and more each day, Beth wondered what evil she had done for God to inflict these injuries upon her. Strangely, she never asked God Himself. She hadn't prayed since the accident happened — not for answers, not for help, not to thank Him for letting her survive the crash. Beth still thought of herself as a religious woman, but she had pushed God away as she had pushed away so many friends and family members she just couldn't bear to see when she was such a mess.

Beth popped two pills. She tried to wash them down with a swallow of tea, only realizing too late that the tea was still searing. She spit it and the pills into the sink. *You damned idiot. You can't even manage to take painkillers without hurting yourself.* Beth shook her head.

***

Frank and Jack returned and took their seats at the kitchen table. Jack began wolfing down his lunch, not waiting for his sister to sit with them. Frank waited, though, and rose to pull out her chair for her.

"Is everything all right at work, Jack?" Beth asked.

"Yeah," Jack said through a mouthful of chewed beef. You remember Don O'Keefe, right? My buddy that I used to go moose hunting with? I was talking to him the other day about the fire. Told him that a Canadian was coming down to do another investigation. He said he'd keep his eyes and ears open for me. Good man. He called to say that he had a lead. Something about a bar on New Gower Street. I know the place," Fowler said. "It's called The Dock — a real hole in the wall."

Beth turned to place Frank's tea in front of him and caught him sneaking a look at her legs. It had been a long time since she saw a man looking at her that way.

"Some tea?" she asked.

Frank looked up, embarrassed. "Oh, thanks," he said.

"Not a problem," Beth said with a smile.

Chapter 12

Wolfram sat on a log he planned to later use as firewood. An upturned helmet sat between his feet. He was using the helmet as a basin, dabbing his combat knife into the soapy water within and bringing it back to his throat. He glided the blade over his skin, removing several days' worth of stubble. It was a rough way to shave, but he had become used to it. Around him, his men busied themselves with preparing the camp. They were being as quiet as possible, but with so many men working, there was still more noise than he would have liked.

He examined their surroundings and noted that so many of the trees were now bare this late in the season. He wished that they weren't. His team could use the coverage. At least there were still some evergreen trees around to hide them.

He closed his eyes and let his shoulders relax. The gurgling waters of a nearby brook filled his ears. If it had been peace time, he would have liked to sit by the brook and fish to pass the time. But this war wouldn't allow for that serenity — not even in a place like this.

These reflections were broken by the clattering from inside the cottage. As Krupp had told them, the site marked on his map had a shelter. It was run down and its interior was a complete mess. Still, staying in the cottage was better than sleeping in the outdoors, and it did something to help hide them.

He noticed that two of his men were missing from the camp. Wolfram turned to Manfred, who was sitting on a flat rock to his left. Manfred was pulling gear out of his pack and searching its insides for something.

"Where's Wilhelm and Einhard? I haven't seen them lately," Wolfram said.

"Remember when you told them to go scouting last night? They found a small lake only a few kilometres from here. They are inside the cabin, getting ready to go there again to hunt fish."

"To *catch* fish," Wolfram said and grinned. "Not to hunt them. To *catch* them." Wolfram pointed at the brook. "Manfred, do you see that stream over there? Stop digging in that bag and go over there. Check the water's quality. I want to be sure we can drink it. And try to catch some fish too. Maybe the villagers around here get their fish from there. If so, then we can too."

Manfred paused as if he was about to say something. He even opened his mouth and then promptly closed it. He nodded to Wolfram, stood up slowly, and walked away. Wolfram clenched his teeth the same way he did whenever he smelled something foul. He saw none of the zest that formerly marked Manfred's character. All he saw was indecisiveness and sluggishness. There was no place for either on Wolfram's team.

When they left for St. John's the next night, he would leave Manfred behind to guard the camp. Wolfram could always deal with Manfred after the mission was complete. For now, he couldn't risk having him ruin the whole operation at the moment its main stroke was executed.

As insurance, he would leave behind a second man to watch Manfred as much as to stand guard. He would choose a tough member of the team, someone who was unfriendly to Manfred. Einhard would do. He was about as mean a bastard as Wolfram had ever met. He didn't seem fond of many comrades, and certainly not someone like Manfred. A few months earlier, the two men almost came to blows and probably would have if Wolfram hadn't intervened.

A rustle came from the bushes behind Wolfram. He didn't need to look at any of his men to know they had heard it too. All sound within the camp ceased.

He turned his ear towards the sound and tried to tune in. The sound was low, but unmissable. From the corner of his eye, he saw two of his men leaning towards the sound. One man slowly reached for his submachine gun.

Wolfram saw a figure taking shape through the trees. The figure's lower half was obscured by the bushes, but the upper half was clear enough that they could see the noisemaker was human. After the figure took a few more steps, Wolfram could see that it was a man in about his mid-forties lumbering through the underbrush.

Over one shoulder hung a bag with a pair of rabbit's paws sticking from the top. A break-action shotgun hung, cracked open, over his forearm.

This hunter moved towards them but did not seem to have noticed them yet. His concentration was on the underbrush, or rather, on keeping his balance as he stepped through it.

The man continued towards them. Wolfram heard him brushing through blueberry bushes, occasionally snapping a branch. The hunter was almost upon them, but still, his eyes fixated on the ground as he picked carefully through the knee-high undergrowth.

Even without his break-action shotgun, the hunter was a threat — certainly not as dangerous as a soldier or policeman, but he was still a threat. One report to the authorities and the mission would be blown.

Wolfram's mind raced to find a solution. If they held him captive, they would have to guard and care for him. Could he spare the men for that? They could kill him. But whether they kept him or killed him, the villagers would come searching for him in these woods.

A rifle shot rang out from Wolfram's right side. He jumped to his left. He swivelled his head to see the shooter while still trying to hold the hunter in his peripheral vision. At his right, Wolfram saw Einhard shouldering his rifle. He worked the weapon's bolt — *clack clack* — and expelled the spent cartridge. Tendrils of smoke crawled from the rifle's chamber.

"Einhard, I never gave you the order to fire. You fool!" Wolfram barked.

"I had no choice. He was going to see us," the soldier said.

"Do you know what you have done? They will send a search party once they realize this man is missing. They will find us and this mission will have failed!"

"We can leave now," Einhard suggested. "Set ourselves up someplace else."

"They will still find the cottage," Wolfram snapped. He pointed to the rickety little cabin. "They will know someone has just been in there."

Wolfram sneered and snatched his sidearm. He pointed it at his own soldier and said, "I could kill you for this." His furious finger pulled back the pistol's trigger, and in that moment, Wolfram truly believed the finger would continue to pull until it placed a bullet through that stupid bastard's heart. Still, Einhard neither attempted to protect himself nor showed fear. Wolfram pointing a banana at him would have had about the same reaction.

"Sir, don't. A second gunshot is definitely not what we need if we want any chance of staying hidden," Manfred said.

Wolfram recognized the sensibility in these words and relaxed his trigger finger. He took a breath and heard some of the men sigh with relief. He holstered his pistol to show that he had regained his control.

Turning to Manfred, Wolfram said, "The only hope is to hide his body and misdirect the authorities into thinking that he is perhaps dead but his body cannot be found. Manfred, you said something about a lake, did you not?"

"Yes, sir."

The hunter groaned, as if wanting to complicate Wolfram's plan. The men looked as surprised as Wolfram to see that the man was still alive. The hunter lay on his back, immobile, but his groaning continued.

Wolfram looked to Einhard and said, "You were the one who shot him. You finish him. Spill as little blood as possible. We are going to have to carry that big fellow deep into the forest. The less blood we leave behind us, the better."

Einhard nodded and removed his wire garrotte from his pocket. He walked over to the wounded hunter and knelt beside him. Without a word of comfort or apology, he got on with business and strangled him.

Chapter 13

Time passed. Jack had arranged for a spare desk to be moved into his office. Frank had been putting it to good use since long before dawn broke that morning. His files were spread like playing cards in a game of solitaire. Most of them he had reviewed three times. He had never been studious before he joined the military police. Now he believed that time spent with his nose buried in records was rarely wasted.

He kept running over the basic details of the case. The fire started in a storage room. It spread quickly to the countless rolls of toilet paper, towels and blankets that were stacked in there. Police figured someone may have left a cigarette butt burning in the room, or committed some other such careless act. After all, the storage room had no cooking apparatuses and there was no evidence of faulty wiring.

All the reports, witness accounts, and letters were giving him a firm sense for the case's details. People's names, their roles, and dates were all sticking in his memory. He was making the connections between them a little faster with each passing hour.

The work was quickened by Tobin's help. The young constable was handy for answering easy questions and fetching files. He had even agreed to take a seat at the desk and fix some papers that had been put in the wrong order.

It was a simple task, but one that would have stolen precious time away from the core work.

Frank glanced at Tobin. The young constable's high cheekbones and gentle jawline contrasted with Jack's hammy face. Frank grinned as he realized this, thinking that Tobin had the kind of face that Frank would have called pretty on a woman. But the delicate features made Tobin look elfin, and his small stature didn't help.

Frank's mind trailed from the work only to reflect on the recent lunch at Jack's house. After eating, the three of them spent time getting to know each other. They sat in the parlour and listened to the radio over extra cups of tea.

Frank was most interested in Beth. She was a looker, no doubt about that. But she also had a strangeness that appealed to him. It was there in her accent, in her conversation, and even in her table manners. It wasn't exotic, as such. She was too humble to be described with such a mysterious word. She was colourful.

He especially enjoyed listening to her and Jack speak to each other. Their speech was fast, and their words abbreviated, but Frank was able to catch most of it. After a week on the island, he was starting to develop an ear for the Newfoundland dialect, what his mother would have called *casual English*.

It had taken a while for Beth to really open up to him. He wished that she wasn't so embarrassed about her arm. He wanted to know what had happened, but he thought it was best to let her tell him in her own time. He definitely wanted to spend more of his time with her and give her the chance.

Jack stepped into his office with a cup of coffee in each hand. He passed one to Frank and said, "So, are you getting anywhere in the fire case?"

There it was again — Jack calling it *the fire case*. Not the *hostel* case. It was as if there was only one fire anyone in St. John's could remember.

"It's coming together. Starting to take shape. You want to grab a stack of papers and help Tobin and me make sense of this?"

Tobin patted his hand on the desk's top. "Oh, Sergeant Fowler isn't a great lover of paperwork, that's for sure!" he said.

Jack shot Tobin a look that Frank figured would have quieted the devil himself. Jack then placed his coffee mug on the bookcase and planted his wide rear on the edge of the desk.

Jack looked at Frank and said, "Remember a while ago when I told you I got a tip about a bar called The Dock? I'm going there once it opens this evening. I need to talk to a guy named Brendan Stockley about his involvement with the hostel. He's a bartender there, but he also worked at the hostel, on the side, pouring drinks."

"Right. I read about him in one of the reports. He was questioned along with all the other employees, but nothing panned out. You think he might have started the fire?"

"No, I checked him. He doesn't have a motive. No record either. His alibi looks solid. I think he's clean, but do you remember reading that part about how he lost his hostel keys?"

Frank sifted through the folders. "Yeah, it's in here someplace. He reported it to his boss, and his boss mentioned it in an interview with investigators afterwards. I don't think I saw much else in the files about that."

"Yeah, that's the problem. There wasn't any follow-up with Brendan himself. They only spoke to his boss. A guy has keys to the hostel. They go missing. A couple of weeks later, the place burns down…"

"And nobody bothered to ask him about it! Jesus Christ!"

Frank saw Tobin shifting in his seat at the end of the desk. He knew that he was making Tobin uncomfortable, but he didn't care. He had to call it as he saw it.

Jack sighed, "I know. It looks like someone slipped. It happens sometimes with big investigations. Something gets told to one investigator, and then he doesn't share it with the others, or it does get shared and others don't think it's worthwhile to pursue."

Frank didn't try to hide his annoyance. "Well, it's a pretty big deal, don't you think, Jack?"

"Don't talk to me like I don't know that it matters, b'y."

Frank felt his face grow hot, but he knew it wasn't Jack's fault that a mistake was made. He supposed they were lucky Jack had caught it now.

Frank sighed. "I'm sorry, Jack. I apologize. Anyway, there's no definite link between the keys and the fire. Maybe he dropped them while working the hostel. Maybe the guy lost them in between the cushions of his armchair and they're still there. Could have been lots of things."

Jack stretched his back and placed his hands behind his head. He let out a heavy sigh, but Frank saw that it wasn't a sigh of frustration. His partner was now deep in thought. Frank watched Jack's eyes flit around the room, not stopping to focus on anything. It was an involuntary reflex from Jack's brain running its analysis. His eyes finally stopped darting around and they flashed to Frank.

"Well, anyway, it was shoddy investigative work that I'm going to fix today. I can see one possibility in particular, and I hope to God I'm wrong. I'll tell you all about it once I've got some coffee in me. Tobin, hand my mug over to me, will ya? I put it on the bookshelf by you."

Tobin turned around to fetch the coffee, but his arm brushed it from the bookshelf. It left a streak of coffee over several books before smashing onto the floor.

Jack belted, "Tobin! Look at the goddamn mess you made. Shards all over the fucking place, b'y! And my good books are stained all to fuck! You clumsy idiot!"

"Hey, why don't you ease up on him?" Frank said.

"Why don't you mind your own business?"

Frank slowly stood up out of his chair. Jack may have been wider than Frank, but Frank was three inches taller. "You bully people like that in front of me, then you make it my business," he said.

Jack grimaced at Frank. "Forget it. It's just coffee. Hold on now. Let me get a mop." Jack stormed out of the office. Frank heard Tobin exhale. Frank was getting accustomed to Jack's rude gestures. They were nothing more than little confirmations that Jack was an asshole. But after being in the office for several days, it was clear that the outbursts meant much more to Tobin.

He turned to Tobin and said, "Hey kid, why do you let Jack pick on you like that? You should stand up for yourself."

"I don't know. I guess he has enough reasons to dislike me as it is."

"Oh? Why's that?"

Tobin shifted his weight and shuffled his feet slightly. He looked away from Frank when he responded. "Sir, my family is well off," Tobin said. "I'm not saying that to be arrogant, but it's a fact that I have to be honest about."

"And Acting Sergeant Fowler doesn't like having a rich man's son around?"

"Something like that, sir."

"I bet some of the high-ranking members of your police department are from wealthy families."

The constable chuckled. "That's different. In Fowler's eyes, those rich men are where they are supposed to be — at the top of the heap. They're not some rich kid like me at the bottom. He has to look at me every day, and I keep getting in his way. Plus, he has another reason not to like me."

"Oh, really?"

Tobin leaned forward and whispered, "Some months back, he had an altercation with a very wealthy man. That man had some influence with the constabulary's top ranks. Next thing he knew, Sergeant Fowler was demoted to *Acting Sergeant* Fowler. The rich man who landed him in hot water also happened to be a close friend of my family.

"I can see that. Rich people in a small city like this are a close-knit bunch. It's hard to imagine pissing off one and not the rest."

"Fowler's not out of the woods yet. There's an internal investigation surrounding the whole thing. He may get sacked from the constabulary yet."

"Jesus Christ. They really put the Nelson on him, eh?"

Jack returned from the kitchen with a mop in one hand and a bucket in the other. Tobin reached for them.

"No, that's all right, Tobin," Jack said in a subdued voice. "I'll clean that up myself." He hadn't looked at Tobin when he spoke, but Frank guessed that was about as good of an apology as Tobin would get. Maybe that was as good as anyone ever got from Jack Fowler.

"So, Jack, when are we going to follow this lead to New Gower Street?" Frank asked.

"*I'm* going to follow this lead. Chasing suspects is beyond the boundaries of your work on the fire case. You're supposed to be reviewing the material already collected and basing your evaluation on that — not snooping all over God's green fucking acre." Jack said.

"I won't. You do it. I'll just tag along."

Jack sighed. "Jesus, I can't wait until you get on that plane and fly back to Nova Scotia or Alberta or wherever you're from. All right, grab your coat. We got places to go."

Frank sprang out of his chair and gathered his belongings. Jack reached into his desk's drawer and withdrew a short-barreled revolver. He checked that it was unloaded and then removed a box of ammunition. The gun looked ridiculously small in Jack's ham-sized hand.

"That's a Colt Detective Special, isn't it?" Frank said. "Kind of tiny, don't you think?"

Jack reopened the revolver's cylinder and loaded in cartridges. "Don't let the size fool you," he said. "It's made small to be concealable, but it's a .38 calibre, and it'll do the job."

Tobin added, "The only drawback with a short-barrelled pistol like that, to my mind, is its poor accuracy beyond short range."

"Toby, you turnip-headed imbecile, the fog on the island is thick enough that you'd never try to shoot anything beyond twenty feet."

Tobin laughed, despite being insulted, and when Jack saw it, even he let a grin crawl across his face. Frank guessed that maybe Jack didn't dislike Tobin as much as he would have people believe.

Jack tucked the .38 into a coat pocket and headed for the door. Frank was one step behind him.

Chapter 14

On their uphill trek towards New Gower Street, Frank took a deep breath and decided to take a chance with Jack, "So, about your sister? I was thinking—."

"Buddy, don't you mind my sister. You stay away from her. Given the last arsehole who left her, I'd say she has enough problems attracting a decent man without a bad one standing next to her. So, you just keep your mind on your case, you got me, b'y?"

Jack had done it again — called him "boy" even though he guessed Jack was only seven or so years his senior. He didn't like it, but it seemed like all men on the island were called "boy" no matter their age or where they were from. He would have to get used to it.

Frank didn't say anything for a while; instead, he quietly studied the streetscape. Occasionally, a telephone pole or fire hydrant disrupted the barren sidewalks. Each object had a white stripe painted on it. He pointed at one, but before he could ask, Jack said, "The white marks are to make it easier to see them when driving around at night. You know with the blackout and all, you can't see a damn thing, especially on moonless nights."

"The blackout must make it hard on people living here."

"The blackout isn't a big problem. After a couple of months, you get used to it. What the blackout doesn't help is the crime problem. The darker it is, the more chance of people getting up to badness ... and the less likely that we'll have any witnesses afterward. It used to be that you could walk anywhere. Now you need a pass to get around." Jack laughed and added, "Trust me, where we're going, it's dangerous enough without getting into a car accident."

Once they reached New Gower Street, Jack exclaimed, "Welcome to the roughest street in North America, b'y. It's not a hard equation to understand. Servicemen from all over God's green acre come here because it's where all the taverns and clubs are. Servicemen with money are going to attract women, including prostitutes. Women attract even more servicemen, and the cycle repeats.

"A lot of fights start because there's always a shortage of girls and way too many men. Not regular men, mind you. They're men trained to fight, to be aggressive. They all just pulled into port, either coming back from the fighting, or they'll be heading for it as soon as their ships raise anchor. These men want to drink, screw, and have a good time. But it goes far beyond that. Two nights ago, a US Army private busted a full Scotch bottle over a police constable's forehead. Put him in the hospital with a fractured skull. We still don't know if he'll be able to resume his regular police duties. He may have to be given a desk job, cataloguing evidence, filing paperwork, or something like that."

"If foreign servicemen are taking all the girls, I bet the Newfoundland men have something to say about that," Frank said.

"Damn right they do!" Jack exclaimed. "It's not the only source of tension between civilians and Allied forces either. We have several militaries stationed in and around the city. They're all providing their own brands of security and intelligence service. This has led to many Newfoundlanders being made suspects in their own country. There's been a lot of inappropriate searches and seizures of property. Unlawful interrogations too. Regular people have been swept up and detained for no valid reason."

"You don't sound too heartbroken about that."

Frank shrugged. "I don't like seeing my countrymen and countrywomen treated this way. But we live in dangerous times, sir. We all need to make adjustments and sacrifices."

"Some more than others," Frank added, thinking about the loss of Jack's son. Still, he wondered if Jack would feel the same way if he were a civilian who had just been roughed up by someone else's army or navy. Frank doubted it.

Engine planes roared overhead. In the darkness, Frank couldn't see any planes, but he had a hunch as to what was flying over him.

"Air patrol?" he asked Jack.

"Air patrol. They fly from Torbay, the same place where you landed, and head out to sea."

"Do air patrols ever sink anything?"

"Damn right they do. Last month, air patrols out of Newfoundland spotted and sank two submarines. And in July, a plane out of Nova Scotia sunk another one. That's a hell of a lot better than what they were getting before. And even when they don't sink any subs, at least having air patrols overhead helps keep the U-boats submerged. They don't work so well underwater."

"Subs don't work as well when they're submerged? How do you figure?"

"Well, just like whales need to come up for air, subs need to surface now and then to air out their chambers and to recharge their batteries."

Frank nodded. "I can see how the air would get pretty stale inside one of those things."

"The main problem is that there isn't enough of those air patrols. That's a big ocean out there, Frank."

"For sure," Frank said and thought about how he had surveyed the ocean during his flight to the island.

From New Gower Street, Jack led the way down a narrow set of concrete stairs snuggled between two houses. Frank wouldn't have noticed these steps and was glad to have a local cop as his guide in the mission.

Chunks of concrete had been gouged out of the steps, and the surrounding walls were marked with crude graffiti. The stairs twisted around overgrown bushes that had sprung through the holes in the steps. As Frank made his way past, he wondered how any city hall could let any part of its jurisdiction fall into such disrepair, even a half-hidden stairway like this one.

They landed in a red-bricked alleyway. A thin view of the streetscape at the alley's opposite end showed busy traffic of both pedestrians and vehicles. Frank assumed that their destination lay there and the bar was, in fact, not as close to New Gower Street as he had understood.

He was surprised when Jack stepped around a fire escape to open a door in the alley's wall.

"In here," Jack said. "It's a booze can. Don't drink any of what you see here. Cheap piss. I'll take you out after this to a sensible bar up the street."

"Christ, Jack. When you said this bar was a hole in the wall, I never thought that you meant an actual—"

"Pipe down. You'll get off on the wrong foot with these people. Let me do the talking," Jack said. He motioned for Frank to move inside.

The wooden staircase creaked as they climbed to a second-storey room. A whole wall of the room was taken up by the bar. The opposite wall held large double windows that filled the room with what little light the streetscape had to offer. The light exposed the crude collection of whaling harpoons and farm tools that hung on the walls. Frank couldn't decide if the sunlight helped to cheer up the bar or make it look worse. A side door led to the fire escape that they had passed below moments earlier.

The bar was only half full, but its small size and the billiards table in its centre made it feel crowded. When Frank and Jack entered, everyone turned to look at them and no one bothered to hide their stares. An unspoken tension — the kind felt when strangers enter a close-knit bar anywhere — rippled across the bar.

Frank saw everyone looking him over and was surprised that no one tried to hide their stares. "Wow, friendly place," he said.

"Remember, we're not looking for any trouble," Jack said. "We'll just get the information that we're wanting and then we're gone."

Jack jostled up to the bar. Frank stayed five feet behind him. He would let Jack talk to whomever he chose, while he watched the rest of the bar.

The patrons were an equal mix civilians and servicemen. They were the bar's regulars — drunks who had been coming there for years and people who were new to the bar (and after this war finished, would never come back again).

He heard an American soldier with a thick southern accent telling a British sailor about how miserable the weather was in St. John's. Replying in an accent, equally thick but Scottish, the sailor told the American that it reminded him of Inverness.

There was a man sitting at the bar's end. He turned his head away when Frank looked at him. The man's ash-coloured suit draped his shoulders in the way that only expensive suits can. His matching fedora sat on the bar top, giving Frank a good look at an expensive haircut. Next to the fedora was a gold cigarette case that caught what little light there was in the dimly lit bar. With his wire-rimmed glasses, he looked like a college professor, the sort of fellow who would drink cognac while dining at the club. Frank thought he must just be a well-heeled drunk, finding booze wherever he could.

Frank turned his attention back to his partner and saw that Jack had already found their guy. Brendan Stockley was behind the bar, leaning forward to take Jack's questions. Brendan was shaking his head, which Frank took as a bad sign. He stepped forward to better hear the conversation, and a blonde man bumped into him.

"Sorry, sport." Frank said, but the blonde guy wasn't listening. Like Frank, he was tuning into the conversation at the bar. The chat drew forward another bar patron. Like the blonde guy, he was a civilian, but this one had dark, greasy hair. Frank didn't like the attention that Jack's conversation was getting. Maybe Brendan would answer the questions differently now that he had a growing audience.

Brendan raised his voice. "Listen, I don't know anything about the fire, other than it was a catastrophe. Thank God I wasn't working that night."

"Well, I need to know more about what went on, not just that night, but in the nights leading up to it," Jack said.

"I told the police about everything that I know already! I lost my keys. I reported it to the hostel's management. And they said they would get me a new set. So, I needed to count on other staff to let me come and go from the hostel and open the inside doors."

"The interior doors, you mean? Like one to a storage room?"

Brendan looked at him cautiously and fidgeted. Frank could almost hear Brendan's heart skipping a beat.

"Yes, along with the other interior doors and some lockers," Brendan said. "I think most people now just want to put it behind them. And you can include me with them."

The dark-haired man took a step towards the bar and said in a hoarse voice, "Is this guy bothering you, Bren? Because we can clear him out of here for you real fast if you want. You damn newsmen can't leave that story alone, can you? Making money off of other people's bones is what you're doing."

"Hey, settle yourself, b'y," Jack said. "We're here on official business." Jack reached for his identification. But placing his hand in his coat for anything was enough to set the dark-haired man into action. He threw a vicious fist into Jack's mouth and pounced on him.

Frank reached to grab Jack's attacker, but then felt hands on his own shoulders.

The blonde man pulled Frank backwards. The pair stumbled and crashed to the bar's floor. Frank eagerly gripped the blonde guy's shoulders and felt them explode with energy. His assailant was quicker than Frank.

Both of his hands snaked to Frank's throat. Frank's whole body tightened when his windpipe clamped shut. After some very slow seconds, he finally wrenched the man's hands off his neck.

Frank knew he couldn't let this fight stay on the floor. Even if he beat the blonde guy, another attacker could jump into the fight. Frank would be helpless if he was still down.

They were both quick to regain standing positions. Frank and the blonde guy squared off with only a few feet of space between them.

Frank's eyes darted up and down, taking the man's measure. The blonde man was shorter than him. Though it was difficult to tell under his layers of clothes he was wearing, Frank guessed that he had a narrower build than his own, and his confidence rose.

Boxing had been a part of Frank's self-defence training, and he had been better than most of the other trainees.

Frank took a boxer's stance, putting his chin down and holding his hands in front of his lower face to protect the ever-precious jaw. He saw uncertainty in his blonde's eyes. Perhaps the attacker was realizing his mistake by going to fisticuffs with a trained man.

Frank's body re-enacted the swift boxing footwork and rhythm that he had once performed so fluidly in the ring. After two steps, he bumped into a stool and tripped. He cursed himself for not seeing that the tight space of a bar would not allow for a boxer's dance.

His recovery was too slow, which cost him a fist to his left eye. Stars flooded his vision. He staggered backwards, but at least that put distance between him and his attacker. His opponent rushed in for the knockout blow, and Frank barely managed a half-step to his left. That second punch grazed his forehead.

Frank slowly circled to his left. His opponent matched him, circling to his own left. The blonde guy stepped forward and cocked back his right arm to launch a looping haymaker. But that movement was slow, so it telegraphed the blow — Frank saw it coming the moment his attacker had jerked his arm backwards.

Frank let the haymaker sail over his head. He then countered with a left jab, landing squarely on his opponent's nose — his head snapped like a book folded over backwards. His chin came up for half a second, which gave Frank the chance he needed to land a follow-up right cross. His opponent's lower jaw snapped shut. Disconnection swam across his face and he fell to the floor. Frank knew he had knocked him out of this fight. He stood over him in disbelief — he had knocked people unconscious before, but not that quickly.

Frank snapped from his trance and spun towards Jack to see how he was handling his own foe. He saw that his boarish partner fought like the beast itself — in close and vicious. Jack alternated between throwing body blows and short hooks and upper cuts. He pressed his hammy shoulder into the man's chest and plowed him into the plaster wall. The wall caved inwards, and the man was left sitting with his bottom wedged inside of it. He tried to pull himself free, but Jack didn't let up. He jerked his head upwards into the man's jaw, snapping his mouth shut, his upper and lower teeth clopping together. Frank winced. He caught the distress in the man's eyes just before Jack landed his elbow into one of his sockets. The poor bastard crumpled to the floor, with Jack landing rabbit punches to the back of his head while his attacker was on the way down. The Newfoundlander did not fight the gentleman's bout, but Frank couldn't deny his effectiveness.

Jack's chest heaved. He wiped a spatter of blood from his upper lip. Catching his breath, he said, "Well, I told you that

I would show you the nightlife. Now let's get out of here before the police show up."

"We are police!" Frank cried.

"I mean, the other kind who would want explanations. I know a place down the street where we can get a drink."

The two men strode for the door. As they passed Brendan, Jack extended an arm and dug his stubby fingers into the back of the bartender's head. Jack pulled Brendan towards him and yelled into his ear, "You're coming with us, arsehole!" He then pushed Brendan towards the stairwell.

Poor luck was an understatement. The night had only just begun, and already, they had gotten into a brawl. At least Frank's supervisor back in Canada didn't know what the hell was happening. Frank touched his right eye. He could already feel his eye starting to swell up.

As they left, Frank cast a last look at the semicircle of speechless bar patrons. No one impeded their exit. And the wealthy man in the grey suit, who had been sitting at the bar, had disappeared.

***

Jack led Frank and Brendan to a pub two minutes from The Dock. Frank knew it was a safer place, not just because his partner had chosen it, but because there were a few ladies inside — Frank reasoned that men are better behaved when women are present.

They settled at the bar, with Jack and Frank sitting on either side of Brendan. Frank didn't care if their bloody clothes and scrapes raised questions. He had worse problems than prying strangers. By the time they had a couple of pints in front of them, Frank's eye was badly swollen.

Jack lit a cigarette and inhaled deeply. He spoke as he blew out the smoke. "Well, that couldn't have gone worse," he said. "We got into a fight with a couple of civilians, and we have nothing to show for it except bruised knuckles. Let's hope that all of our dead ends don't end that way."

"I'm not so sure that it was a complete loss," Frank replied. "Brendan, there was a guy at the bar. He was wearing a grey suit and glasses. Who was he?"

"Oh, that was James Kelly. He's an Irish guy. One of our beer suppliers. Sells to a lot of places around us."

"He looks pretty well off for a beer distributor."

"He doesn't just distribute. He's got his own brewery and everything."

Jack inhaled deeply again, but this time, he released the smoke out in one long blow and said nothing. Frank saw that Jack had caught onto his game. He would let Frank ask the questions while he tried to get a second read of Brendan's responses.

"Does he come in a lot?" Frank asked.

"I don't know. I guess so. Comes in a few times a week, so I suppose that's a lot."

"You talk to him much?"

"Yeah, I talk to him. I talk to everyone. Rubbing elbows is part of a bartender's job as much as fixing drinks."

"You ever talk to him about the hostel?"

"A few times"

"What did you tell him about the hostel?"

"I don't know. Can't remember."

"But he knew you worked there."

"Of course. He knew that much. A lot of people at the bar knew that. Listen here, I never had anything to do with that fire. I mean, maybe some things about Kelly may seem queer now, when you start adding in everything else you said, but at the time, everything was all right. I mean, he seemed all right, so I'm innocent, right? Please tell me I never had anything to do with that fire."

The mix of pleading and desperation in Brendan's eyes was hard to bear. How could anyone carry the guilt of knowing they were an unwitting partner in such a heinous crime?

Frank placed a hand on Brendan's shoulder and gently said to him, "Most times people find themselves in trouble, it's because they absent-mindedly walk into it. Hindsight always tells them that they could have avoided it if only they had kept their antenna up."

Brendan swallowed and closed his eyes. Frank was glad to see the young man was taking relief in those words. Brendan finally opened his eyes and gave Frank a nod. Whether it was a sign he understood what Frank had said or that he was grateful for the comforting words, Frank couldn't tell.

"Hey, I need to get out of here. If I'm gone from The Dock too long, after what just happened, I'll lose my job for sure."

"Go on. Get," Jack finally said.

As soon as Brendan scurried off, Frank said, "James Kelly. I have a bad feeling about him."

"I'm listening," Jack said.

"Well, it's a damn good cover for an enemy operative, isn't it? A beer distributor? The guy travels from site to site, one pub to the next, eavesdropping on conversations, meeting new people from different lines of work. They share their stories, they're all in places where a few drinks can lower their guards and loosen their tongues. And the whole time, it doesn't look that strange to anyone. Kelly is just a guy delivering for his brewery, right? That's not exactly the sort of job that police and intelligence normally keep an eye on."

Jack nodded, and Frank thought he caught a look of admiration. He may very well be impressing the tough piece of shoe leather sitting across from him.

After gulping from his pint, Jack said, "I take your point. You know, you're right. It is a good cover. It doesn't hurt that he's Irish either. Newfoundlanders are a little friendlier to the Irish than they are to most foreigners. Sorry, no offence."

"None taken. And here's a strange thing — he seemed very interested in us, but when we left the bar, I didn't see him anywhere. Everybody else in the place was frozen watching the show we put on. But he disappears? I think things were getting a little too hot for him."

Jack lit a cigarette and inhaled deeply. Frank could tell that Jack was rolling around Frank's ideas. "I wouldn't mind learning more about that guy either," Jack finally said. "Just after the war started, the constabulary started keeping a full list of aliens. I'll check out the files and see what I can find out about our new friend, Mr. Kelly."

Jack downed the last of his pint and signalled for two more. This was in spite of Frank still having a half pint in front of him. Frank didn't object. He thought the alcohol might ease the throbbing in his face.

He saw that Jack was looking past him. He looked over his shoulder and saw a group of soldiers sitting at a table in the corner. The oldest couldn't have been more than twenty-one. They were raising their glasses and cheering. Maybe they were happy to be Europe-bound. Maybe they were happy to be coming back. And maybe they had just found out that they had gotten lucky and wouldn't have to go over there to fight at all.

"That brings back memories. It's hard to believe the Great War ended almost twenty-five years ago."

"You sound like you're talking from experience. Did you serve?"

Jack raised his chin and said, "I was in the Newfoundland Regiment. It was hard living in those trenches. Looking at unburied bodies and living in lice-ridden clothes. But my God, weren't we all ever proud to be part of the regiment?"

"You know, I never enlisted because I was bored," Jack continued. "I knew some boys who thought that the biggest event in history was happening in Europe, and that they were on the wrong side of the Atlantic. They went over there because they thought it was all a lark. Just one big adventure for boys who had never seen a town bigger than St. John's. No sir, I never had time for such foolishness. I served because I thought it was a noble cause — fight for the glory of the British Empire. To do my share to uphold what we had all built together. I wasn't about to let the Germans, or anyone else, take it all away from us without a single shot fired. Now, so long after the bloody war ended, they've taken my son. He was the most important thing to me, and I never got off a shot this time."

Frank wriggled in his seat before straightening his posture. "I saw the letters back at your house. Beth told me about your son. My sincerest condolences."

"Thank you, sir."

"You know, you don't have to—."

"No, it's all right. Some people have told me that talking about it might help."

Frank asked, "And what about Billy? Why do you think he went over there?"

Jack sighed, and for the first time since Frank had met the Newfoundlander, he looked tired — no, exhausted. "My wife says that he enlisted because of me," Jack said. "I filled his head with ideas of fighting for king and country. Duty to the crown and all of that. Perhaps she's right. Maybe he's gone now—."

The absence of Jack's wife from the home now made complete sense to Frank. He had heard that the death of a child strains a marriage like few other things, but what happens when one parent blames the other for the child's death?

"But I think my wife is wrong. I think my son saw the war for what it is."

"And what's that?"

"This war is different. It isn't a fight for the Empire or for nationalism. The war is a battle for mankind. I know how that sounds. People killing people for the sake of people. But I mean, it's a war to decide what shape humanity will take."

"Maybe you're right. It could be. But either way, Jack, you can't blame yourself for what happened to your boy. Billy made the choice to go over there to fight, and I think *it was* for a good cause. This war is different from the last. It isn't a fight for the Empire or for nationalism. Hitler, and people like him, have led humanity to the brink. This war is a battle for civilization's soul. Will we fight for what we've built as a people — a species — or let civilization disappear altogether?"

Frank took a long pause followed by a slow drink from his pint. Frank was starting to feel foolish for the speech he had just given, but then Jack finally spoke.

"I get you. It's just a hard thing for a father to reconcile," he said. "It may take me some time."

Frank understood that. So without a word, he patted Jack on the shoulder. He had no children, but he didn't need any to make sense of Jack's words. Jack looked at him. Frank saw that all of the coarseness had gone out of Jack's eyes. It had been replaced with warm gratitude.

Frank downed the last of his pint and slid his untouched one towards Jack. "Here, you drink that. I'm going to start on something heavier than beer."

A smile brightened Jack's face. "Frank, I'm starting to like you."

Chapter 15

The wind blew through Wolfram's light sweater. He put on his coat and closed it tight. Wolfram had read that winter comes in fast in Newfoundland, but he still hoped the worst of the weather would wait until after his team had been extracted from the island. Still, that autumn wind felt more like a winter gust. He looked up to the clouds and wondered whether they would drop rain or snow on them tonight. He didn't need a weather station to know that the worst was yet to come.

The operation had been delayed. Wolfram had wanted to move into St. John's days ago, but moving around the woods while it was filled with search parties was too big of a risk, so his team was forced to stay hidden. Furthermore, they had consumed almost all of their meagre supply of emergency rations, and the search parties had prevented them from foraging in the wilderness for food. If only that careless oaf, Einhard, had not shot the hunter.

But now, the search finally seemed to be relaxing. As well, his scouts had reported that the remaining searchers seemed to be focused around the pond, a few kilometres away.

A gust blew a wet leaf against his face. He brushed it away and took it as another sign that he had to move now. Days weren't getting any warmer. And only God knew when another damn hunter would stumble upon them. He was certain his team couldn't simply make a second one "disappear" as they had the first.

He called the men into a huddle. "Pack up your gear. We leave for the city in one hour." I want us to travel as fast as possible to compensate for the time lost. That means that we keep the team as small as possible. So, I want two men to stay here and guard the camp. Manfred and Einhard, you will be staying here. The rest of you, bring only what's absolutely needed. We've trained for this, and you all know what you will need to do once we get there. Get to it, men."

The huddle broke apart and each man set himself to his tasks. Except for Manfred. He stepped towards Wolfram and said, "No medic this time, Captain?"

"No medic this time. I told you what I wanted. Go get your aid kit ready, Manfred, and prepare a space for the wounded. When we get back here, we will probably have some. Go on, you are wasting time here."

As soon as Manfred left, Wolfram stopped Einhard from cleaning his submachine gun. Wolfram pulled him close and said. "Keep an eye on Manfred. I am not saying there is anything wrong with him—. Just watch him. Be certain he does not do anything stupid. Anything that may hurt us."

Einhard nodded and Wolfram patted him on the back. Einhard might have been reckless, but he was a reliable soldier that Wolfram could count on to shoot Manfred, if needed.

With another heavy gust, the wind beat against Wolfram's face. He removed his wool hat from his coat's pocket and pulled it snugly over his head. Soon he and his team would be in St. John's.

Chapter 16

Gong ... gong ... gong.... The clock hanging near the room's entrance marked ten o'clock. Frank opened his eyes and struggled to remember where he was. The bird-patterned chesterfield underneath him was as unrecognizable as the room's tea set and modest coffee table. The folded clothes on top of the coffee table, however, he did recognize. They were the clothes he had been wearing the previous night, except cleaner and neater. They appeared — somehow — to be freshly laundered.

He was in someone's parlour. The room certainly had all the usual markings of a parlour, except for the boxes. In one corner, there were stacked boxes of assorted items. Shoe polish, chocolates, shaving kits, pocket combs, and other small objects.

The memories of the previous night came flooding back to him. Most of them, anyway. After the bar fight and far too many drinks, Frank agreed to spend the night at Jack's house. The chesterfield short for a man of Frank's height, but given the condition he'd been in, he was ready to sleep anywhere.

He didn't need to touch his eye to know that it was very swollen, but he did anyway. The bulge under his bottom eyelid was sizable, but his cheek was even worse — it felt like a golf ball was stuffed under his skin. It hurt to poke it, but he did anyway. He had a hell of a headache, which he attributed more to the alcohol he'd consumed than to the fight.

Frank heard the lazy sizzle of bacon frying. He peered down the hallway and saw Beth setting the kitchen table. He pushed himself off the chesterfield and shuffled out of the parlour. With each step, the air became greasier, and his stomach began to grumble. He needed water first.

"Good morning," Beth said, smiling but not turning away from the kitchen table. "You two came in late."

"Yeah, good morning. Mind if I get some water?"

"Help yourself. So, where did you boys go?"

"Chasing a lead on … New Gower Street, is it?"

She giggled. "Oh, I see. I suppose you got a good look at the city at night. Something, isn't it?"

"You can say that again."

"I can tell you this much — when this war ends one day, life in St. John's won't go back to the way it was before the war started. People here have had a taste of real, modern living — new entertainment, better buildings, more goods on the market. They'll want to keep it all."

She turned to him and gasped when she saw his eye. "Oh my goodness! You did more than see the city. I can get you a cold cloth to put on that. It'll help with the swelling."

"That's okay. It's not my first black eye. Is Jack up yet?"

"He left for the station hours ago. Jack said he never wanted to wake you. He told me to fix you something when you got up. How crispy do you like your bacon?"

"Forgive me, but I don't think I have time for it. My apologies. It looks pretty bad if he's at the station, and I'm still at his house eating breakfast."

"Oh, he's not at the station. He called about an hour ago. He said that you'll have to work your fire investigation alone today. He's been temporarily placed on another duty. A hunter has gone missing in the woods, and he's helping with the search."

"Whereabouts exactly?"

"Not too far from St. John's. In a little place called Seal Cove. I know that you're new to the city. Maybe there's some things I can help you with today. I could be your guide. I could—."

"That's okay. I think I can figure things out by myself. Besides, your brother might not be comfortable with me taking you along on an investigation."

Her face hardened, and between stiff lips, Beth said, "I'm not some blushing teenage girl afraid her father won't allow her to see a boy. I'm a grown woman, b'y. I can take care of myself. Jack don't get to decide who I spend my time with."

Blood rushed to his face. "I'm sorry. I didn't mean to offend you. Of course, I would love it if you came with me today. We can leave as soon as we eat some of that fine bacon."

He poured himself his second glass of water and sat at the table. Beth scooped heaps of bacon and fried eggs onto his plate. She smiled; he smiled back. He hoped that he had smoothed over that rough patch.

"Say, I noticed those piles of shoe polish and socks and things in the den. What's that all about?"

"Oh, I volunteer with the Red Cross, down at the hostel. A big part of the job is putting together these little bags. 'Comfort bags,' we call them. They're for the survivors from the submarine attacks. These poor people are delivered from sea to dock, and we're standing right there when they come in, to give them whatever they need."

"Which is?"

"Which is everything. Clothes, food, medical care, a warm, dry place to stay. Love from somebody. After what they been through, they need love from anybody."

"Yes, and after floating around in the Atlantic for a few days in a lifeboat, I'm sure they appreciate it."

"We try, Frank."

Frank admired her. This woman had her difficulties, but she wasn't a quitter, that was for sure.

Beth's face filled with hesitation. Frank could tell she wanted to say something. He patiently waited. Finally, she said, "Frank, I think … I know … I can help you with your investigation."

"Oh?"

"Since I volunteer with the Red Cross, my supervisor lets me take the Cross's car to run errands. We can use that to get around the city. I know you can't do your work by just sitting in an office. You need to get outside and do things. Well, if your work is anything like my brother's, you do."

Frank chewed his lip. "I don't know about that," he said. "I *do* have to watch someone today, but the idea of tailing someone in a car as conspicuous as a Red Cross station wagon, that doesn't appeal to me."

Beth's eyes brightened. "Then again, who would ever suspect a Red Cross station wagon?" she exclaimed.

Frank cocked an eyebrow. "I hadn't thought of that. You're right. It might work out for the best this way. So, you want to grab your boss's car without permission? Won't you get in big trouble for that?"

"I'll risk it, if it means helping you and Jack. Let's go!"

Chapter 17

Exhilaration flowed through Beth. She wanted to place her hand on her chest to feel the quick heartbeat. Her limbs trembled. Even the fingers on her right arm were tingling. If she'd known detective work was what she needed to get more sensation in that arm, she would have made Jack take her to work ages ago. Beth wanted to smile, but she knew that any sign of her girlish excitement would only reinforce Frank's idea that her participation was a mistake.

They climbed into the station wagon. The heavy vehicle was light green with the Red Cross emblem painted on its wooden doors. Like so many other vehicles on St. John's roads, the headlights of this one were covered in black tape, and only a tiny gap in the middle of each headlight to let small beams through when needed.

Frank did not object to Beth's driving. She supposed that, back in Canada, he was used to driving on the right-hand side of the road, so maybe he found having to drive on the left foolish — or perhaps too confusing.

He did a poor job of hiding his embarrassment of riding in a car driven by a woman — something that finally did make her smile.

It only took ten minutes to drive out of the downtown and arrive at their destination. Beth and Frank sat in their ambulance, parked in a lot adjacent to a small brewery. Their position gave them excellent coverage, and a narrow view of the brewery's entrance. They began an exercise that Frank called surveillance, but to Beth, it felt like they were just watching the building's entrance.

After two hours, the wait was becoming uncomfortable. Beth was now regretting the second cup of tea she had had at breakfast. She hadn't thought about the inconvenient demands of her bladder on a stakeout. More importantly, the painkillers that she had taken just before they left were starting to wear off. She wanted to take more, but not in front of Frank.

She was about to ask him if they would wait there much longer, when their man emerged from the brewery. James Kelly, Frank had called him. He hadn't told Beth much else about him other than he was Irish and he owned the brewery.

A cigarette dangled from Kelly's lower lip. In his left hand, he held a fancy cigarette case, which Beth guessed was the same one Frank had mentioned to her on the drive over here. His three-piece tweed suit fit him so well that she knew he must have a good tailor.

"He's awfully fancy for a man who owns that tiny brewery, isn't he? I mean, I expected to see a regular man. A working man."

"Yeah, that's one of the things that caught my eye about him. Nice car too. It looks brand new," Frank said and pointed at the Chrysler in the brewery's parking area.

The man got into the car and drove for the downtown. Beth and Frank followed. There was little traffic to hide them, and Beth was trying to keep extra distance between their vehicles. Their target parked his car near Water Street and headed in that direction. Once he exited his car and took five steps, moving behind a building, they lost sight of him.

"All right, we've lost him. Now what?" she said.

"Now, I go after him," Frank said.

Beth opened her car door.

Frank said, "Beth, what are you doing? You're *not* coming with me."

"I'm not coming with you. I'm going instead of you. Think about it. He's already seen your face at the bar, swollen eye and all. But if this man is looking over his shoulder, a woman with her arm in a sling would look harmless. Come on, Frank. You know that I can get closer to him than you can without getting caught."

Frank chewed his lip — a habit she found adorable. Beth could tell he was carefully considering her words. She knew he wouldn't have a good argument against what she had just said. She also knew that for a man, a good argument still wasn't always enough.

She was about to add that if her brother found out she tailed a suspect, she would tell him that it had been her idea. But she kept silent. She knew how proud men could be in front of each other. Her comment might be taken as a suggestion that Frank was afraid of her brother. If Frank interpreted it that way, he would be turned off from her idea completely.

Frank grudgingly nodded his consent. Beth sighed in relief. A grin split across her face. Suddenly, her back pain didn't feel quite so bad.

James Kelly was in no hurry to get to wherever he was going, and that gave Beth the time she needed to chase after him and catch up. While closing the distance between them, she stepped behind a crowd of men and two women who were moving in the same direction. She stayed close enough to them and hoped she would appear as if she was part of their group.

Kelly stopped in front of a grocer's stand that took up a small section of sidewalk. He perused the selection of garden vegetables but didn't once look at the grocer behind the stand.

Beth broke away from the crowd and stopped at the vendor too. She smiled at the grocer and asked for some fresh carrots and turnips. She hoped that she was inconspicuous — just another regular shopper buying groceries. Despite the seriousness of the task at hand, she allowed herself to feel some pride in what she thought was a smart move.

While the grocer placed the vegetables in a paper bag, she watched Kelly in her peripheral vision. He leered at her, eyes moving up and down, sizing her up. She hoped he wasn't noticing anything other than her figure.

Finally, Kelly left the stand and continued along Water Street. Beth carried her groceries and stayed several steps behind him. He walked faster; she matched his pace. She realized Kelly might be testing to see if she was following him. She slowed.

Kelly entered a café. Beth stopped herself from following him through the door. Instead she walked past the café for thirty steps and then circled back towards it.

She didn't need to be inside to picture the café's interior. She knew the place well, as she had been going there for years. The place was larger than one might have guessed from its narrow storefront. A front area contained a counter and a few tables. But near the room's rear, a short hallway led to a spacious back room.

As she entered, she was greeted by the smell of burnt coffee and the sounds of busy conversations. She could see that the front room was filled with customers, but she didn't look among them for her target. She headed for the counter and waited in line. Lineups were unusual for this spot, but she saw the reason why. A new member of staff stood behind the counter and struggled with a cash register as it refused to open. The customers waiting ahead of Beth shuffled their feet and loudly sighed.

It was only after she received a cup of black coffee that she searched the front room for her man. Kelly wasn't there, so she moved to the back room. She found him as the room's lone occupant, sitting next to one of the café's rear windows. In a quiet corner, he reviewed a notebook. He studied its contents with such interest he seemed not to notice her. She sat as far away from him as possible and began to rummage through her grocery bag, as if her carrots and turnips were of great interest too. She wished she had a better set of props to work with. Any moment, he was going to lift his head from his book, see her, and … and what then?

Beth found her courage and reminded herself that it was her idea to get involved. Indeed, she insisted that she be a part. *No one put a gun to my head*, she told herself.

She took a deep breath and reached for her coffee. She took a long gulp. It burnt her tongue, but she forced herself to swallow it. She stole a glance at the Irishman. He frantically scribbled in his notebook. Beth would give her right arm to know what was driving that frenzy (not that her arm was doing her much good these days anyway).

He looked away from his book but not at her. He leaned towards the window's pane and rested one hand on the sill while sipping his coffee with the other. He surveyed the harbour. Beth thought that the Irishman must be doing some spy work. There was certainly plenty of naval activity for him to share with his spy bosses — or whoever he reported to. Then she saw him smile and a look of incredulity filled Kelly's eyes. Beth realized that the man was not watching the harbour for any sinister reason. Rather, he looked as amazed by its liveliness as everyone else in the city. He seemed to even be admiring it. It was the same look of astonishment that Beth saw on Frank's face when he spoke about the harbour during their first meeting.

A second man walked into the room. Being the only other people present, Beth wondered if the two men were there to meet. There was something familiar about the newcomer. The man removed his hat and Beth recognized him as Constable Tobin Aylward. She had met him a few times when she had visited her brother at the police station. He was a timid man who was made even more so by Frank's constant browbeating.

As awkward as the situation looked, Beth was certain that the presence of the two men in the same place was a coincidence. St. John's wasn't that large of a city. It wasn't unreasonable that a police officer and a suspect would happen to show up in the same café. Was it?

But Tobin was quick to open a copy of *Time* magazine and pretend to read it. All the while, he peeked over its edge to study Kelly. The constable's actions were obvious to Beth, so she concluded that it wouldn't take the Irishman long to notice his new observer.

Why don't you just cut out some bloody eyeholes in the newspaper to stare through? she thought.

She knew that she had to get Tobin out of the room but had no idea how. Kelly was still transfixed on the harbour below them, but Beth knew that wouldn't last. If Kelly was what Beth expected he was, any moment he would notice the bonehead policeman sitting not thirty feet from him, watching him with all the discretion of a steamroller at a garden party.

Kelly downed the last of his coffee and he pocketed his notebook. As he strolled out of the room, he checked his handsome wristwatch.

Beth wanted to ask Tobin if he thought their target had seen either of them, but of course she knew she couldn't. Besides, she saw that the constable was transfixed on the Irishman and was trying to peer at him through the room's doorway. From what she could tell, Tobin never once looked at her.

You don't see me either, she thought. We've met a few times before, while my brother was chewing you out, but you don't see me now. I'm invisible to you.

It was best to leave it that way for now, and let Tobin make the next move. She sipped her coffee and began rummaging through her purse. She figured that was good cover, since no man she knew would take any interest in a woman rummaging through her purse. To her, it looked more ordinary than searching through her bag of vegetables.

Tobin rose from his chair and hastily exited. Beth waited a few moments before doing the same. Through the shop's front window, she barely saw the edge of the constable's coat before it disappeared behind the corner. She moved after him.

A three-way chase was on now — four-way if Frank was to be counted. She wondered where he was and what he was making of all this. He was probably regretting the whole situation. It wasn't what she or Frank had expected, but it wasn't like this sort of thing could be planned either.

She had almost made it through the front door when a bolt of pain electrified her. Beth's back stiffened into a rail of agony. She reached for the nearby countertop and leaned her weight against it. She bit her lip and stifled a cry, but it hardly mattered. Customers had already noticed. Some rose from their seats to help her. The girl behind the counter reacted quickly — she raced around the counter to Beth's side and lightly placed her hand on Beth's upper back.

"Are you fine?" the girl asked. "Please, missus, come over and sit down."

"Yes, my love, sit down," a man's voice called from his table. His weathered face showed genuine concern. Beth cringed and managed to give the elderly man a weak smile.

There wasn't anything Beth wanted more at that moment than to sit down, but Frank was counting on her to follow Kelly. She closed her eyes and remembered her doctor's advice. She took deep breaths, letting them out slowly, and waited for the pain to subside.

For a second time, the old man called for her to sit down.

"No, I can't," Beth said. "Thank you, but I have a job to do."

"It can wait. Whatever it is, it can wait for you to get yourself right," the man said.

"No, not this. Thank you for worrying all the same," she said. Between grappling with her pain and tottering towards the door, she didn't look once at the man.

She made it out the door and turned left. Neither Kelly nor Tobin were in sight. She scanned across Water Street but found no clues as to where they had disappeared. There was no sign of Frank either.

Her best guess was that the Irishman was making his way back to his car and the constable was still tailing him. She headed down the sidewalk and hoped that she was making the right move. Her pain was receding, and her stagger faded to only a slight shuffle. Still, at that pace, she would surely lose them. She forced herself to walk faster and took tortured breaths every few steps.

She moved rapidly, the whole while guessing how long it would take Kelly to enter his car, start it, and pull onto the street. Could she close the distance between them in that time? She had to hope and push herself a little harder.

The pain returned, but now only in the middle of her back. Her muscles tightened. It felt like a horse had kicked her there. She cursed herself for not taking an extra dose of pain medicine before she and Frank had set out on their little adventure. The whole thing now seemed hopeless. She was no Nazi hunter. How could she think that she could make a difference to something so important?

She would have walked past the alleyway on her left side if it hadn't been for the shouting. She wheeled around and towards it suddenly enough to send a fresh jolt of agony through her torso. Through watering eyes, Beth peered down the tight lane that ran between two brick buildings. At its end were Tobin and Kelly gripping each other in a deadly wrestling match.

It looked like the Irishman was getting the better of it. The constable's legs were buckling under him. Kelly's chubby hands choked out what little resistance Tobin had left. Even from the other end of the laneway, Beth could see his eyes rolling into the back of his head and his face flushing with colour.

Beth gave one glance around the streetscape to see where the hell Frank was. He wasn't in sight. There was no time to wait for anyone else to help. The young constable had only seconds left before unconsciousness overtook him. Kelly had beaten a police officer, and she wondered what chance she had against him. But she had to try.

Beth dashed down the lane faster than she would have guessed she could. She was barely aware of her pain now. Beth sprang onto Kelly's back like a wolf on a moose. Her one arm laced around his thick neck while her right dangled unresponsively. Less than a second later, Kelly's broad back exploded against her chest. His neck thrashed, and she could feel hard muscles pressing against her forearm. Beth hadn't realized how strong a man could be until she tried wrestling one. But at least he released his grip on Tobin's throat.

Before she could dismount Kelly, he saved her the trouble. A pull with one arm sent her ass over applecart into a pile of trash. A discarded bed mattress broke her fall. It took her a moment to recoup, which Kelly used to gulp down huge breaths of air. He placed his hand over his heart and slumped against a brick wall. Beth could tell he was light-headed. If she could only keep that massive heart of his racing and his massive lungs fighting for breath, he would collapse in another minute. Maybe less.

She pulled out of the garbage, but the effort brought her pain back. A spasm struck her with the force of a hammer just below her shoulder blades. Her cry was cut short by Kelly's backhand lashing against her cheek.

Beth didn't remember falling to the ground. She only knew that she was down. Stars filled her vision. She heard voices, but she couldn't recognize them. They sounded muffled — like people trying to scream under water.

A boot brushed against her side. Someone had kicked her. No, someone had accidently bumped her. It happened again. She turned her head to the left and saw two men wrestling above her. It took her a moment to recognize them. It was her adversary fighting Frank. *Where the hell were you?* she wondered.

She saw that Frank had pulled out his revolver and was trying to aim it at the Irishman. But Kelly held Frank's gun hand with both of his own. A violent shake sent the pistol to the ground. It clattered and bounced next to Beth. She strained to reach it.

Finally, she clutched the revolver and aimed at Kelly just as he threw Frank to the ground. Kelly stood over Frank and raised his right foot, ready to stomp. Another moment and Frank's teeth would be ground into the back of his head.

"Stop!" Beth cried. Kelly turned to her. It took him a second to realize what she was holding. She aimed the gun at the man's chest. "I don't need two working arms to pull a trigger," she said.

Kelly froze and stared at her. His shoulders heaved from exhaustion. His mouth hung open, partly to draw greater breaths and partly in disbelief.

The distraction gave Frank the time he needed to recover. He grabbed a length of rusted pipe from the trash pile. He brought the pipe down on the back of the Irishman's head. Beth saw Kelly's eyes bulge outwards. She thought Frank had hit him hard enough that he had knocked Kelly's eyes out of his head. Then Kelly crumpled to the pavement.

Frank rushed next to her side. "Are you all right, Beth? Are you hurt?"

"Yes, but no more than usual." Despite the pain, she managed to smile. "We did it," she said.

"No, honey. You saved me. *You* did it."

Chapter 18

Frank pushed Kelly through the doorway of his own house. He could have let the man walk into his own home, but Frank was in the mood to shove. Not only had Kelly assaulted police officers, he had hurt Beth. That was an offence much less forgivable. Beth had been commended to Tobin's care. Her injuries from her car accident didn't seem greatly aggravated by the alley fight. The scrapes she had sustained were minor. Tobin had assured her that there wasn't anything wrong with Beth that some calming tea, ice, and rest wouldn't fix. Tobin himself seemed well enough. He was surprisingly calm for a man who had almost been choked into unconsciousness — maybe even killed. That impressed Frank. Perhaps Constable Tobin Aylward was made of sterner stuff than Frank had thought.

Jack followed both men inside the home. He had been oddly quiet ever since he received Frank's phone call about the alley fight an hour earlier. Frank had assumed his hot-tempered partner would have kicked Kelly's teeth into the harbour by now. Instead, Jack had hardly spoken. He only watched. His pale-green eyes never left Kelly.

"Are you all right?" Frank asked. Jack still said nothing. But when Frank placed his hand on Jack's shoulder, he felt Jack's muscles trembling.

Frank had noticed that in what few words Jack had spoken, he had not once called Beth his sister. Frank doubted it was an oversight. Jack didn't want Kelly to know that the woman he had fought with in the alley was a relative. It wasn't a bad idea for Jack to try to keep his sister as far out of this mess as possible. No one knew how big the German operation was or who was connected to it. The less they knew about Beth, the better.

It had been Jack's idea to bring Kelly back to the man's own home. He figured they could interrogate Kelly while searching his place for clues.

Frank figured he would leave the interrogation to Jack. And since Jack didn't need spectators to beat answers out of Kelly, Frank began ransacking the apartment.

He started with the bedroom. People always like to hide things there. Searching the dresser drawers yielded no clues either. That wasn't a surprise. If Kelly owned anything that linked him to the Nazis, he sure as hell wouldn't leave it next to a stack of his underwear. He would have found a secret place for it.

He next grabbed the bed's mattress and flipped it over. Under the bed frame was a revolver. This made sense. If Frank were connected to the Germans, *he* certainly would keep a gun under his bed too.

Frank picked it up and inspected it. The pistol was an antique, but Frank guessed it could still do the job. He opened its cylinder and checked to see if it was loaded. He unloaded the bullets into his hand and placed them and the revolver into his coat pocket. Anticipation raced through him. The investigation was taking giant leaps forward.

He began pulling down the pictures from the wall and checking the backs of them. It took only two checks before he found a large brown envelope taped to the back of a landscape painting.

"I found something!" he yelled and started to make his way back to the kitchen. From the hallway, he heard Kelly curse.

"Shut up, you bastard," Jack replied. "Shut up, or I'll give you another good goddamn crack."

As he entered the kitchen, Frank tore the envelope open. Inside was a thick stack of bank notes in various national currencies and an even thicker stack of photographs.

Jack snatched the photos from Frank's hand and splayed them across the kitchen table. Both men studied the images before them.

Many shots contained warships or busy servicemen backdropped by low-level buildings. These matched Frank's memories of the city's waterfront.

"Are these shots of St. John's Harbour?" he asked Kelly.

Kelly nodded. "Yes, but I didn't take them. A German fella took those and told me to hold on to them for him."

"A German fella?! We'll get to him in a minute after I get a better look at these." Frank looked closer. He could make out the flags and other insignia of naval buildings. In one picture, a pair of sailors were smiling and enjoying their conversation, completely oblivious to the German photographer who couldn't have been too far from them. Frank had to give the spy credit. He must have been very good at his trade to have gotten so close undetected.

Frank shuffled the photos around the table and even saw several shots of that ramshackle fishing village within the city — The Battery, Jack had called it. From a military perspective, it was barren and boring. There was nothing of interest, save for the US Army supply dock, which he could make out in detail. He remembered how Jack had said the new supply dock was a real attraction. But to Frank, it was nothing special.

"Jack, do you recognize anything?"

Jack nodded. "This picture here is from the beach in Conception Bay. I can tell from the islands in the background. So is this one here. And that one too."

Jack grabbed Kelly's ear and twisted hard enough to make the Irishman howl. Frank prayed that Kelly wouldn't put up a fight. There was no telling what Jack would do in his current frame of mind. "Why all the pictures of Conception Bay?" Jack asked. "What's so special about the bay? Tell us!"

Kelly snarled at them. "I'm not telling you anything. Aren't you supposed to have some sort of papers before you can search my home? Some legal docu—."

Jack's fist crashed into Kelly's jaw. The blow's force was great enough to send the back of Kelly's head against a cupboard door. If Jack hadn't grabbed Kelly by the throat, Frank was sure that the Irishman would have gone to the floor.

"There's your fucking papers. Do you want an extra copy?" Jack said and raised his fist.

"Hey! You can't do this. I have—."

Another blow landed against Kelly's cheek. "Quit that nonsense, b'y. We want to know about the hostel fire. Don't you dare tell me that you don't know anything about that."

"All right. Okay. I'll talk."

Jack lowered his fist and Kelly sighed in relief.

Kelly began. "I was doing my rounds one night, going from one tavern to the next. I stepped out for some fresh air and when I was around back, a man came up to me and asked for a light. I got talking to him. He said his name was Sam Wheeler. I got to know him. You know, just from seeing him on my rounds. We would sometimes sit and have a couple drinks together. He seemed like a decent enough guy. I confided in him, a few times, over pints. I told him what I thought of the war and the Crown. I told him that Hitler could have the whole bloody Empire for all that I care."

"Oh yeah, and what did he have to say about that?" Jack said and spat on the kitchen floor.

"Eventually he told me that his real name was Krupp and that he was German, though you would never think so from the way he talked. He sounded like he was American! Krupp started asking me for information, and he told me he would always pay a pretty penny for it."

"And it all really started from there, right?" Jack said.

Kelly groaned. "Krupp's mission in Newfoundland was to gather information on what he called 'targets of opportunity.' He was the one who took those photos, not me. He never planned to destroy anything or hurt anyone. Well, that's what he told me anyway."

"I see," Jack said and breathed deeply. "And eventually, you got around to doing some favours for him? Like stealing a key to the hostel from the bartender at The Dock?"

"Yes."

Jack snapped, "So, you're telling us that this guy Wheeler or Krupp or whatever the fuck his name was set fire to the hostel? That bastard killed a lot of innocent people. You know that, right?"

"Yeah, but you can't pin none of that on me!"

An emotional helix formed within Frank — anguish, rage, betrayal. His brother's terrible death Frank wouldn't have wished on anyone — and this scum had helped kill him.

Frank struck Kelly — the hardest blow the Irishman had received yet. The punch landed against Kelly's left eye. He couldn't have seen it coming — couldn't have braced himself for the impact.

Kelly fell out of his chair and lay like a starfish on the kitchen floor. Lying spread as he was made Frank think he had knocked Kelly unconscious, but that didn't stop him from launching a verbal assault on him.

"You piece of shit! My brother was in that hostel when it burned."

Kelly only shook his head from side to side and moaned. His eyes were closed. Frank wasn't sure if his words had even registered with Kelly, which also aggravated him. He was about to say more when Jack interrupted.

"Enough of this. We got Germans to catch. Let's get out here."

"Any idea what we do with him?" Frank asked and pointed down at Kelly. "It was your plan to bring him back to his place. What do you want to do with him now?"

Jack chewed his lip and his eyes shifted away, which Frank could only interpret as a bad sign.

"You don't have a plan, do you, Jack? All right, let's drop him off at the station."

"We can't bring him to the station."

"Why not?"

"The only advantage we have right now is that the Germans don't know that we're on to them. We can still move on them quietly, assuming we don't ruin our chance by calling up the whole police force. I don't want to tip off the rest of the constabulary to what's happening. I'm guessing that the Germans have their ears to the ground. If they sense that the police are mobilizing for an operation to find them, who knows how they'll react! Let's just keep it quiet for now."

Frank nodded. "You're not thinking of letting him go, are you?"

Jack balked. "Fuck, no! Do you think I'm mad? Just keep your mouth shut for a minute and let me handle this."

Frank stepped back and took a deep breath. There was nothing else for him to do but wait to see what Jack would do next.

Five minutes later, the semi-conscious Kelly lay handcuffed to the railing of his staircase.

"Don't worry, you backstabbing turd. You won't be like that for very long," Jack said to him. "While we're out dealing with your arsehole Nazi friends, why don't you think about a good legal defence? You're going to need it."

Kelly scowled and said something, but his words were muffled by the gag in his mouth. He pulled against the rail and cursed them with his eyes.

Jack turned to Frank and said, "After we catch his friends, we'll move this joker into a jail cell. I'll contact my friends in the British Security Service."

"You think they have a record on him?"

"An Irishman who's working with the Nazis? I'm counting on it!" Jack said. "Once the Brits get involved, I guarantee you that one way or another, he'll be taken off the constabulary's hands. Not our problem after that."

"Well then, come on, Jack. We're wasting time here." Frank gestured towards the front door. "Do you really think we'll get back to him soon?"

"Frank, we'll find the Germans soon enough, and I promise that Kelly will be out of those cuffs an hour later. Or…"

"Or what?"

"Or the Germans will kill us. In that case, Kelly won't be your problem anymore."

***

As Frank closed the front door, he heard a vehicle pulling into Kelly's driveway. He turned to see Tobin parking a constabulary squad car. Through the windshield, Frank saw Tobin giving him and Jack a comforting nod. It appeared that the young man had done a satisfactory job of caring for Beth. Frank guessed she was back in her home, resting in the parlour he'd woken up in that morning. He pictured her drinking some herbal tea and resting under a wool blanket. Frank smiled. Good. She'd earned the rest.

Thinking of Beth cued him to address another matter. Frank took a deep breath and prepared to make his apology to Jack. Frank hadn't forgotten about how he had put Beth in danger. He was damn sure that her brother hadn't forgotten either. He would have to do it sooner or later. It was just as well to get it out of the way now.

He turned to Jack and said, "It takes a big man to—."

Frank's apology was cut short by Jack's blow to his face. It sent him reeling against the door with a heavy thump. Tobin slammed his car's door and took a step forward to interject. Jack shot him a look that was enough to put Tobin's ass back a step.

Jack glared at Frank. His eyes burned with anger. "You son of a bitch! That was for my sister!" Jack howled. "What were you doing? If you wanted to follow a suspect, you should've waited for me! You don't know the city well enough to find anyone in it. And how could you do this to her? You put an infirmed woman in harm's way! And

I'm not stupid, b'y. I know why my sister would want to involve herself in your investigation. You've found your way to her bed!"

Frank tried to object, but the accusation was more of a shock than the punch he had just taken. His words froze in his throat and stayed there.

"*Partners*, you called us," Jack continued. "You wouldn't know what the word means." He spat on the ground and clenched his fist, as if he might throw another punch, but he restrained himself. He lowered his arm. Then he lowered his head. And for half a second, Frank thought he saw a tear in the brute's eye.

Tobin finally stepped forward and spoke softly. "I'm sorry, Jack. We never planned it this way, and I know you're mad—."

"Damn right I'm mad," he said with a cracked voice. "I'm mad that my son was killed in a damn war that is turning out to be bigger than the one they said would end all wars. I'm mad that lives were lost in a hostel fire, and we aren't even sure what caused it. And I'm mad that they sent in a foreigner to show all of us fools on the island how to investigate the crime because they don't think we could handle anything bigger than a stolen fishing pole."

Jack cleared his throat. "And what about you, Toby, you little Judas. What the hell were you doing there in that street fight? Don't tell me you're sleeping with my sister too!"

Tobin straightened his back and looked Jack in the eyes. "I wanted to show that I could do more than just be your bloody punching bag," he asserted. "I overheard you and Frank talking about your plans to follow the Irishman. So, I decided to go in and see what I could find out for you. I'm sorry for my part in the whole flop."

Frank sympathized with Tobin. He knew what it was like to want to impress one's superiors. And he had seen how Jack treated the young man.

Jack stopped, closed his eyes, and took several deep breaths. It looked like a sort of calming exercise — Frank wasn't about to interrupt. He rubbed his hot cheek, not eager for another bashing. He didn't need Jack to tell him that he messed up either. He had to say something to break the silence.

"You want me to go back to Canada?"

"No, you're here now, b'y," Jack growled.

Chapter 19

Jack had cooled off on the ride back to the station. Tobin and Frank settled with him in his office. Jack sized Frank up, saying, "you may be able to help with the case of the missing man — feller named Gerry Reid — out in Seal Cove."

"Still no sign of him, eh?"

"No body found. There's plenty of signs, though. A search party found his clothes next to Legionnaire's Pond. A flask of alky was next to them. It was almost empty. Looks like Reid got drunk, decided to take a swim, and drowned. We have boats on the water. To add to it, the American navy is in town, so they've even let us borrow some of their divers to take a look along the pond's bottom."

Tobin raised his eyebrows and stepped forward. "Swimming? At this time of year, sir? Well, I suppose it's awfully cold for a swim, but when you're drunk, who knows what you're liable to do."

Frank shrugged and said, "And after all that ... the search parties, the divers ... they still couldn't find him? It's too bad, but at least it sounds like an open and shut case for the constabulary."

But Jack shook his head and grimaced. "No, it's not. If it were, I wouldn't have even brought it up now. I said we found his clothes, right? But there was only one boot. Have you ever gone for a swim, left your clothes in a pile on the shore, but thrown away one goddamn shoe?"

Frank shook his head.

"That's right, you didn't. This guy never did either."

"Do you know what I think, Frank? I think the police are being led astray. I think Gerry Reid's body is in those woods somewhere, but not in that pond."

"Have you told this to anyone else?"

"No. If I did, it might change the direction of the investigation, and I want whoever it is that's trying to fool us to think they're doing a great job of it."

Tobin raised his hand slightly to speak. "But I know that pond," he said. "Grew up not far from there. I can tell you, Legionnaire's Pond pours into a stream that then empties out into Conception Bay. I imagine that the poor devil was flushed out into the Atlantic. He's probably at the bottom of the ocean by now, getting eaten up by lobsters."

"Now that is good speculation, Toby. But my own theory isn't without a base. I talked to a woman who owns a general store in Conception Bay. A Mrs. Ruth Fagan. She said she saw him at least twice a week. She also said that he never bought any booze from her, and apparently, he gave up the alky years ago — reformed drinker. I talked to Reid's wife and she confirmed. Her husband never touches the stuff anymore. Plus, I took the bottle of booze they found at Legionnaire's Pond. Said to the other b'ys that if Reid was drowned, there'd be no harm if I finished it off myself."

"Oh yeah?

Jack reached into his coat's deep pockets and removed a small canvas bag. He gently opened the bag and pulled out a half-finished flask. The label was torn, but Frank guessed the amber liquid inside was whiskey.

Jack handed the bottle to Frank and said, "That's the flask we found with the clothes. I don't think it's done telling us everything it has to say. Take a look. What do you see?"

Frank held the flask close to his face and examined it. The bottle was filthy. Grey dirt was smudged all over the glass, and some large chunks of it were caught between the neck and the cap.

"I see some dirt."

"Not dirt. Clay. It was all over the hunter's clothes too. But there's no clay like that along the pond's shore." Jack leaned forward and lowered his voice, as if he were telling a dirty secret. "But the ground in Newfoundland is so rocky, you understand? Grey clay deposits are rare here. Damn rare."

"I can think of one around here!" Tobin said.

Jack smiled. "Sure you can. Because you just said that you grew up out around that place. I can think of that place too, Toby," he said.

"Are you serious?" Frank said. "You think you know where this bottle has been?"

"There's only one place anywhere near here that has grey clay like that. It's in Conception Bay, near Seal Cove. It's sort of away in the woods. But the people who live within distance of it make use of the clay. Just for crafts and a little pottery — things like that. Over the years, they've even dug a giant pit out of the clay. A hole so big that you can fit a house into it. Why don't we go search it before it gets too dark out?"

"And what do you think we would find there, Jack?"

Jack shrugged. "I'm not sure, but if I had to guess, someone killed this poor bastard Reid in, or near, that big clay hole. Then the killers dumped his clothes and that there bottle down by Legionnaire's Pond in order to throw the cops off the right track."

"So, you think the body is at the clay pit, Jack?" Frank asked.

"Where the body is, Christ b'y, I don't know. I do know that our best shot at finding some answers is to go look for them in that hole."

Tobin looked puzzled, "I'm having a hard time taking it all in," he said. "What are Germans doing in Seal Cove? I grew up there and never met a German in my life."

Jack covered his lighter to block it from the breezy night air. He puffed on his smoke and said, "We're living in strange times."

Frank reflected on his trip to St. John's Harbour. He remembered the big guns trained on the harbour's entrance and how Jack had jabbered on about the many other defences laid to protect the city. He smiled. "Sly bastards. You got to hand it to them," Frank said. "Why would they try to bust into St. John's through its locked front door when they can climb in through the open back window?"

Tobin's brow furrowed, then his eyes widened. "The Nazis are landing in Conception Bay and making their way by land to St. John's!" he exclaimed.

"Jesus, Toby! Keep your voice down." Jack hissed. "We don't need the whole damn city knowing about what's going on."

Frank tapped Jack on the shoulder to bring back his attention. "Forget him for a second. What do you think they might be doing here? I mean, what's worth attacking in St. John's?"

Tobin said, "There's a camp in the city where the POWs are kept. Maybe the Germans are trying to rescue their own."

Jack scoffed. "Sure, where would they escape to? We're on an island of rock and bog."

"I'm not so certain of that," Tobin replied. "If German operators could be landed here on the shore, then why couldn't prisoners be taken off of it?"

Jack shook his head. "I'm not buying it. They're up to something else."

Tobin said, "Maybe they're after the cables?"

Frank raised his eyebrows. "Come again?"

Tobin explained, "St. John's is a communications hub. Several Atlantic cables run close to the city, connecting Newfoundland with New York, London, and other big cities. Damage to these lines would do a heck of a lot to impair Allied communications."

"These cables — they're guarded, right?"

Tobin shrugged. "Their stations are guarded by militia and police officers, but not many of them."

Jack stretched his back and placed his hands behind his head. He let out a heavy sigh, but Frank saw that it wasn't a sigh of frustration. His partner was now deep in thought. Frank watched Jack's eyes flit around the room, not stopping to focus on anything. It was an involuntary reflex from Jack's brain running its analysis.

"I don't know," Jack said. He drew from his cigarette. "I'm coming up with nothing too. Look, maybe we're trying to work this problem from the wrong end. Let's just get out to the pit as soon as we can and see what we can find."

Frank sighed. "Maybe you're right. How many other guys do you want to take to this pit with us?"

"None."

"Jack, I know you don't want to risk tipping off the Germans by talking to headquarters, but this thing is getting out of hand. We need to bring in every cop on this island."

"I can't. Don't you see? I can't!"

Frank dropped his eyes. Jack continued quietly, "I know Toby told you about my troubles. About the internal investigation that's coming. I thought I was just going to get a good scolding from senior command. Now I may be removed from the constabulary. Jesus, how was I supposed to know that rich bastard was connected? Now a career that I've spent over twenty years to build is in danger. But don't you see? If I can crack this case about the missing hunter … if I can stop a German plot…"

"…then you'll be a hero," Frank finished.

"Not just a hero. A hero the world over! There's no chance that the constabulary will get rid of me when I make the papers from New York to London. I'll be too popular with the people for them to expel me."

Frank was in awe. There was no doubt that Jack's plan was selfish. Keeping information from the constabulary at this point might be endangering the public, but nonetheless, his plan could work.

"You clever, self-serving bastard," Frank said. "You may very well save yourself with this long shot. And that's the real reason you don't want to tell anyone else in the constabulary about what's going on. You're trying to crowd out everyone else, so at the end of the day, you'll be the only man standing in the spotlight to get the credit."

Jack only lowered his head. Frank thought he wouldn't speak, but then he finally said, "For now, only you and Toby have the real story. But if the chief gets wind of everything that I've done up to this point, well, you know…"

Frank *did* know. If the constabulary's leadership learned about what had transpired, they would put every officer in the service on the case. Jack would be just one of the many officers then involved, indistinguishable from the rest. After the investigation finished, what then? He would still be at risk of losing his job. Hell, he may also face some prison time. The Newfoundlander had everything to win by keeping his findings quiet, everything to lose by reporting it. Still, Frank couldn't let Jack's secret investigation continue.

"Look, I know you have your troubles, but I can't accept this, Jack. We're telling people."

"Goddamn you! What about the stuff you pulled with my sister? You almost got her beaten to death in that alley. Where was you concern for the public then, when it was your priorities that were at stake?"

It was Frank's turn to be silent. He couldn't argue with that point. Jack took a breath and stepped forward. Speaking in a low voice, he continued, "Look you've gotten evidence of your brother's murder and a suspect who confessed to his part in it. I've helped you tie up that loose end. Now, please, help me with mine. I don't want to see twenty years of my life go down a toilet for nothing."

Grudgingly, Frank nodded. Jack was right. He never would have gotten this far if it hadn't been for Jack's help. How could he abandon him now when Jack needed him the most? Would it really hurt if he spared Jack a day or two to play his hunches?"

"All right," Frank said reluctantly. "So what's your great plan?"

"Thank God you see the sense of it, b'y." Jack's shoulders relaxed, and he exhaled. "Here's my plan: On the front stage, we'll let it look like the search is continuing around Legionnaire's Pond. Toby, your family has some influence with the press, right? I want you to pull some strings and get a couple of stories to the papers. Tell the newsmen that the search for our missing hunter will stay focused around the pond, but at this point, the authorities don't expect to find much. Tell them we anticipate calling off the search very soon. I want those stories appearing on front pages of the next editions, understand?"

Tobin nodded, and Jack turned to Frank. "Meanwhile, you and I are going to that pit, Frank. Right now, I want to get out there while there's still some daylight left."

"You're right. It will be hard enough finding clues, let alone in the dark."

"That's not what I was thinking about. There may still be some Germans in those woods. If they're as smart as I suspect, they'll be hunkered down now, resting. Nighttime is when they'll be awake and active."

"Just like vampires, right?" Tobin said. "They sleep in the day and creep around at night?"

"Yeah, just like vampires. Except that if we put one in a coffin, he'll damn well stay in there."

Chapter 20

Jack parked his car on a dirt road that, to Frank, was identical to the rest of the roads they had passed. He was glad to be with someone who seemed to know the area. A gash of red sky in the west bathed Conception Bay in a burning twilight, animating the roadway and its surrounding forest.

Jack got out of the car, and he brushed off some cigarette ash that had fallen on his clothes during the drive. "This is it," he said. "Do you see that trail over there? We'll walk that for a mile or so, and it'll lead us to the pit."

Even in the twilight, Frank had no trouble seeing the trail his partner referred to. The trailhead was broad enough that four men could walk abreast through it. He guessed that the trail was used frequently for pulling loads by sled. He was glad of that. After all, a well-*used* trail is a well-*worn* trail. They wouldn't have too much trouble making their way through the undergrowth.

Frank reached into his pocket for his cigarettes, but Jack stopped him before he could light one.

"Are you nuts, b'y?" Jack said. "Lighting up smokes in the woods is a good way to get yourself shot. If the Germans are still in here, they'll see the end of your cigarette burning in the dark. They'll see it from two hundred feet, easy. I remember, back in the war, more than one good man getting shot from the German trenches just for making that same mistake."

Frank put away his pack, embarrassed that he had made such a rookie blunder.

The two men made their way for the trail. "What are the chances that we're going to find something?" Frank asked. "Slim to none?"

"It's the slim part that you should be focusing on. Whole wars can be won on slim chances, Frank. Don't forget it. Now, let's hit that trail."

***

By the time they reached the pit, the day had not yet rolled into full darkness. The last of the blessed twilight gave them some light by which to see. Once it became complete night, Frank doubted that the starlight was going to do them much good. The flashlights they had brought would probably remain turned off, since turning them on would make them visible — much like a burning cigarette — to anyone else in the forest.

Still, he didn't need much light to know that the pit's clay was the same colour and consistency as the clay that had been smudged onto the flask. His heart beat faster.

The two men spread out and searched the ground for trash or anything else of interest. Frank searched intensely, all the while, mindful of the day's dying light.

After one hour of searching, Frank was starting to believe the whole trip was pointless. Maybe they should have taken more time to come up with a better approach. But Jack was so damn cavalier. *It's easy to see how the wife would have had trouble putting up with Jack at the best of times,* thought Frank. He immediately felt guilty letting such a mean thought enter his mind.

He was about to suggest they stop their search but thought it would be best to take an extra look around. They had driven all this way and sacrificed a night just to be here. He crossed the pit to a spot still unsearched.

"There! Look!" Frank whispered. Lying only thirty feet away was a dark leather boot. Even in the dim light, it wasn't difficult to spot the boot against the pit's ashen tone.

"Reid's other boot!" Jack said softly. "I knew we were on to something." A smile split across Jack's face. He raced across the clay to beat Frank to it. Jack plucked the boot from the clay and shook his trophy at Frank. "Yes, Frank, that's the man's boot. So it is."

"There's something else, Jack," Frank murmured. "Look at all of those boot prints." Frank pointed to the clay, and there were several prints as neat and well-defined as professionally made casts.

"There's an awful lot of them for one man to make," Jack replied.

Frank snatched the boot from Jack's hand and examined its sole. He ran his hand over the tread and then knelt next to the prints. He turned on the flashlight to check the boot prints better. He was mindful that the light could announce their presence, so he hooded it with his hand. All of the boot prints had the same tread, and Frank had seen enough army boot prints to know their general pattern when he saw it. Their tread did not match that of the hunter's boot.

"What are you thinking?" Jack asked.

"I'm thinking that most, if not all, of these prints were made by someone besides Reid. Someone, or some people, wearing army boots."

He inspected the prints more closely. "I think you're right — all these prints could pass for army boots. I'll check with the army when we get back to the city, but I don't think they're running any exercises in Seal Cove right now."

The two men followed the boot tracks all the way to the edge of the pit where they connected with the opening of a path. The narrow track was overgrown from lack of use, and Frank couldn't see how deeply it penetrated the sea of surrounding evergreen trees. Thankfully, the first shafts of moonlight gave enough illumination for him to see some broken branches that led deeper into a thicket of pines.

To reach the path, he had to step over a large heap of rocks. He was mindful of his footing. One bad step would send him rolling down several feet to the bottom of the pile. He had taken a few steps up the heap when a gentle hand fell on his shoulder.

"Don't walk up there, b'y. When things get in your way, walk around them, not over them. When you walk over things, you raise your body up for anyone else in the woods to see you. Go around."

Frank backstepped down the rock pile and walked around it. This was the second time in less than an hour that Jack had shown him how to keep stealthy. He was glad to have the man as his partner.

They followed the little path for five minutes. Frank heard nothing else but his own footsteps and his own breathing. He drew his revolver. He didn't need to use it, but it felt reassuring in his tense hand.

The high boughs of the evergreens were beginning to block the moonlight, making it difficult for Frank to see. If there were any more cracked branches to follow, he couldn't see them. He sighed and felt his hot breath against his clammy face. He was about to turn to Jack and signal for a break when a pungent odour filled his nose. It was definitely burning tobacco — a cigar or pipe, he thought. Somebody else was here in the woods, and whoever it was wasn't far from them.

Frank's eyes widened, and he looked to Jack. His partner was standing as still as a stalking cat pausing close to its prey. He had smelled it too. Jack reached over and clamped onto Frank's shoulder, and Frank felt the urgency in Jack's grip.

Frank searched the darkness for signs but saw nothing. Jack whispered into his ear, "There. Look closely."

"I don't see anything."

Jack stood behind Frank. He lay his arm against Frank's cheek and pointed again. "Look down my arm," he said.

Frank looked along the line of Jack's arm to the tip of his pointing finger. Seventy yards away, barely visible through the tangle of foliage, Frank saw the end of a cigarette burning in the blackness. The smoker inhaled, and the cigarette flared. Frank's heart stopped. It could be one of them. He always thought of the war as half a world away. But now it could be a real, honest-to-God, enemy soldier standing close enough that Frank could call to him.

Pull yourself together man! Frank's conscience screamed. You need a plan — fast!

They would sneak up to the smoking figure and silently seize him before he could alert any of his comrades. He and Jack were badly in need of intelligence. Interrogating the smoker would be their means to it.

Frank was about to whisper his plan to Jack, when his partner took two steps forward.

"Halt!" Jack cried. "You over there with the smoke! I'm—."

The glowing cigarette plummeted to the ground. A new light burst from the figure's waist. Flashes of yellow were accompanied by the barking of automatic gunfire. The shooter let out a burst so long that Frank was certain he had emptied his magazine. He and Jack dove behind a pair of pines a moment before the trees were chopped by bullets.

If it had been daylight, and the shooter could have seen them better, Frank was certain that he and Jack would have been cut down. Never in his life had Frank been so thankful for the darkness.

"What the hell?!" Jack cried. He unholstered his gun.

The shooter had taken cover as well. Frank searched the darkness for him. He listened for him but heard nothing except Jack's breathing. He wanted to tell Jack to shut up for a moment, but he was afraid to whisper.

Frank surveyed the woods and saw a silhouette rise from behind its cover. The figure shouldered its weapon. This time, Frank knew that the man would not blast off a whole magazine randomly into the night. Instead, he would fire short but accurate bursts into them. *We need a winning move. Fast.*

He levelled his revolver at the figure and fired two shots. The man screamed and fell. Before Frank could assess whether he was alive or dead, Jack moved towards their enemy. Jack sprang from his cover while firing his own sidearm, trying to get in close where his short-barrelled .38 would have a chance at hitting. He was going for the killing blow before the fallen figure could recover.

Frank could make out the body jerking on the ground as Jack's bullets slammed into him. Jack fired and advanced until he stood over the figure. The woods were silent, except for the clicking of Jack's dry firing his empty weapon.

Frank scanned the woods for any other adversaries and then rushed to Jack's side. By the time Frank reached him, Jack was already kneeling next to their attacker. He checked for a pulse.

"Nothing," Jack said. "I can't feel anything."

Frank didn't care. He was too busy diving for the dropped submachine gun. He knew that they had gotten lucky, considering they were armed only with revolvers. He hoped that the submachine gun's additional firepower would give them an advantage over anyone else in the woods. It was an American-issue Thompson. He checked the chamber and magazine before he slung the Tommy gun over his shoulder. He'd received only a brief introduction to submachine guns during his training, but his instructor said he was "a natural" with them. He prayed his training — and luck — would hold up.

"To hell with it, get out your flashlight and give us some light, will you?" Frank said.

Jack risked switching on his light and examined the body. He wore army boots, and a dark coat that could have been green, but Frank couldn't tell for certain in the poor lighting. Frank searched the man's pockets and found no identification — only stubby cigarettes.

"Take a look at those," Jack said and handed the blue pack of cigarettes to Frank. Frank took the pack and turned it over. The French lettering was the first thing he noticed. He removed one of the cigarettes and saw the manure-dark tobacco poking from its top. He sniffed it. The dark tobacco smelled much stronger than the lighter tobacco that he used. He wrinkled his nose. For Frank, that explained the cigar smell. The dead man reeked of it.

"Smoking those is a good way to burn out your throat," Jack said. "I smoked a lot of them when I was in France. That's a French brand — hard to come by in Newfoundland, even before the war, let alone now."

"Jack, forget the stinking cigarettes. Do you know what all of this means?"

"Yeah, I do. Their plan, whatever it is, just had a lot more coal added to its boiler. Whatever they wanted to do, which was probably set for days from now, they'll try for in the next hours. We need to crack these guys tonight!"

"Agreed. We came here to look around, and this guy is proof that there is much more to be found out here. Let's search around here a little longer before we take this back to the city."

Jack nodded, and the two men rose to get back to business.

**

They crept through the woods, staying low and using the underbrush as cover. Frank searched the trees for any signs of Germans. He was certain they had heard the gunfire. They were probably lying in wait for the slightest flicker of movement among the trees to open fire.

It didn't take the two men long to find a cabin. It was situated in one of the few places in the forest that was free of trees and rocks.

Moonbeams gave Frank a full view of the structure. From a distance, it appeared unsuspicious. Its sagging roof gave the first indication of its age. Garbage, partly buried under soil and pine needles, lay around its edges. The cabin's only window had holes through its pane, as if the local boys had gotten bored and chucked rocks through it. The structure sat on stilts, and Frank wondered if it would be them or the cabin's sagging roof that would give way first.

Frank hunched forward and moved while cradling the submachine gun. His heart kicked against his chest. He knew Jack was only a few feet behind, now holding both their revolvers, clutching one in each hand like an Old West gunslinger.

They covered the last yards to the cabin's door in a crouching run.

"I'm busting in!" Jack hissed as he climbed the cabin's log steps.

"No, wait! I'll cover you."

Jack waited until Frank reached the top of the steps, then took a good firing position, kicked open the rickety door and dashed in. Jack waved his pistols at the darkness, searching for a target. Frank peered into the corners of the cabin and didn't see anyone. He concluded that if anyone was in there, both men would have been shot by now.

He heard Jack let out a heavy sigh. "Looks empty," Jack said. Frank could sense the tension leaving Jack's body.

Now inside, they switched on their flashlights. Frank swung his light across the cabin and saw stacks of food rations, cookware, a pair of binoculars, and quite a few wool blankets.

"Christ, it looks like there may be a lot of them."

"I'm more interested in this," Jack said. He waved his flashlight's beam across a radio and a collection of other machines. Frank recognized some of the equipment — a shortwave transmitter and a receiver, but he couldn't identify some of the other pieces.

"What do you think all this is?" Frank asked. He turned the dial of a boxy device, and it began to click.

"Don't touch that! For all we know, it could be rigged to blow up. God knows what the Germans got planned with all these gadgets."

Frank pulled his hand back quickly, like a child who had touched a hot stovetop.

Frank picked up a notebook and thumbed through the pages. He saw technical details for construction —

measurements, materials, time estimates, costs. A sketch of a structure would occasionally appear. Though, at face value, there was nothing sinister or suspicious about the book's content.

"What do you make of this?" Jack asked and handed Frank a different book. The small, leather-bound book contained jargoned letters and numbers.

"This has got to be a code book," Frank said. "I remember them showing us examples of these during our training."

"Can you read any of it?"

"Even if I read German, no. Bring that book with you and protect it with your life, Jack. There's no telling what our cryptographers will learn from it. You know, judging from some of these charts over here, I think this is some sort of weather station."

Jack nodded. "Yeah, I've heard of Germans setting up weather stations in Greenland, and I guess it makes sense that they would try to put one over here sooner or later. But, if this is a weather station, then where are all of the scientists?" Frank said. "That guy we plugged didn't fight like a scientist, that's for sure. Where do you suppose the rest of the Germans are?"

"To answer your question, they've already left for St. John's," a voice cut in from behind them.

Frank and Jack spun in unison. A man stood on the cabin's steps. Both men levelled their weapons at him.

The man raised his hands. He said, "There is no need for that. I willingly surrender."

Chapter 21

"Have you finished interrogating me?" Manfred asked.

"I prefer to think of it as an interview," Jack replied. Frank studied Jack's expression, looking for a hint of humour in what his partner had just said. Jack's snarled lip and squinting eyes held none. Frank was slowly learning that Jack rarely joked about his business.

The German crushed his cigarette butt into the overflowing ashtray. He promptly lit another cigarette. Its acrid smell filled the room. Frank's head pounded. He rubbed his brow. It had been years since his last migraine, but he worried he may have one coming.

The last few hours had been a flurry of activity. It all happened too quickly for Frank to remember in any great detail. He recalled Jack arresting the German, a race to the police station, blurting out the story to a shocked Tobin, and not much else.

Frank glanced towards Tobin, who frantically scribbled into his notebook, though no one had spoken for a minute. Jack had ordered the constable to lean with his back against the office's door, thereby covering the door's small window. Frank guessed that Jack didn't want anyone to see what was happening in his office.

As well, it wasn't overlooked by Frank that Jack had pulled the German into his own office instead of an interrogation room, that he hadn't booked the man, and that he hadn't told anyone about the dead Nazi they had left in the woods. Frank wondered how long Jack could keep the German a secret in a police building — a place filled with experts in finding things out.

Jack had already told the German the list of charges he could be facing. None of these were sticking well in Frank's memory — the only words he recalled were *murder* and *sabotage*. Frank had never liked the sound of that word — *sabotage*. It made the German operatives sound slick and professional, when Frank saw them merely as glorified killers. He wondered if he would recall any of it in better detail later for his written reports. But there was no time to worry about that now. The focus needed to be towards learning what the Germans planned to do next.

Now the four men were together in silence. They had already covered a lot of ground and gotten a hell of a lot of information. Frank was grateful for the break. His brain needed a moment to process. He and Jack stared across a table at the German whose name, he had told them, was Manfred. Frank had done many interrogations before, but none of them were like this one. Normally, suspects denied their involvement and would stall for time. They would request that everything be repeated and ask plenty of questions for which they already knew the answer, all the while trying to think up some sort of plan for defending themselves. Frank always saw what they were doing. Finally, at some point, they would ask if they could speak to a lawyer.

But Manfred, sitting across the table from them, wasn't following that script — not even close. Manfred had already told them a great deal. He had spoken about how the Germans had travelled to Newfoundland by submarine and set up their base camp in the woods. He even told them a little about the hunter who had gone missing. The poor man had stumbled upon them after bagging some rabbits. One of Manfred's comrades had shot and then strangled him.

That's one murder solved, Frank thought.

Manfred was now the quietest that he had been since they captured him. Frank doubted the German was doing this for effect. The circles under his eyes were amplified by his pale complexion. The grey of his eyes reminded Frank of dull pencil tips. Those leaden eyes made the German look even more worn.

Frank doubted that Manfred had been eating or sleeping well these past nights. The cabin in which Manfred had been staying was cold and lacked furniture — rough accommodations even for a German soldier. Since being seated in the interrogation room, the most action that Manfred had taken was smoking that chain of cigarettes.

Jack finally ended the silence. "So, why didn't you and your friend back at your camp go into the city with the rest of your team?"

"Einhard — the man you shot in the woods had the name Einhard — he and me were left to be guards."

"Einhard," Jack repeated slowly and loudly. He cast a glance at Tobin, who quickly scribbled in his notebook. "How many of you are there?" Jack continued.

"There were seven men in our team, but you killed Einhard," Manfred said.

"So, with you now in custody, that leaves five." Frank said, glad to add something to the interrogation.

Jack shot him a look that told him to keep his mouth clamped shut. This was Jack's place, his interrogation room, the world that he knew better than anyone. Jack wasn't about to let the interview be spoiled by an interloper.

"You know, you haven't told us much about that hunter," Jack said.

"The hunter?" Manfred said.

"You know, the one your team killed in the woods. Where is he now?"

"Oh, yes. Him. Terrible. It was Einhard who killed the hunter. That was unfortunate, but needed."

"I don't think his family would see it that way. He had a wife and six children."

For the first time, Frank saw anger rising in Manfred's face. The German's eyes narrowed. He heard Tobin turn a page and his pencil jotted faster.

Manfred stared at Jack for a full minute before responding, "Why did you tell me that?"

"I don't know. It seemed important. Like, if we didn't say it, we would be missing something."

Manfred nodded in agreement. "I suppose. But you see? By telling you all about the hunter, I show that I am not denying anything," Manfred said.

"There would be no sense even if you tried. The evidence against you is too great." Jack's expression reverted to his poker face. "One thing that you haven't told us is why you told us anything at all. You surrendered easy enough. You haven't refused to answer any questions. What about the fight for the German race? What about making Germany the master of Europe?"

"That is Hitler's cause, not mine."

"No allegiance to the Führer?"

The German placed his hand over his heart and said, "My loyalty has always been to the state. But I do not like what I see anymore. I do not like what I see Germany has become. To hell with Hitler. If not for Hitler, the world would not be in flames today. My commanding officer does not share Hitler's vision either. Hauptmann Wolfram is a man of honour.

"Hauptmann Wolfram?" Tobin asked.

"*Captain* Wolfram to us, Toby. He's equal rank to one of our army's captains," Jack said. "And keep your mouth shut and your eyes on your notes."

Manfred added, "Hauptmann Wolfram does not have Hitler's dream of an Aryan race. Certainly does not. And he doesn't believe Germany should be the master of Europe and beyond. But he is still an officer and, like me, his heart is to the state. To Germany."

"We'll get back to your officer in a little while, but you mentioned flames a moment ago. Why don't we talk about those? What can you tell us about the fire at the hostel? We want to know everything you know about that."

Frank's heart leapt at those words. This was it. The hostel fire was the whole reason he wanted this case. This was the engine that propelled him to Newfoundland in the first place!

Manfred took a drag off his cigarette, held its smoke in and then blew it out. "Hostel?" he said. "What is the hostel?"

"The building that burned down with all the servicemen in it."

"Oh, I don't know anything about the fire, apart from the little parts Wolfram told us when he killed Agent Krupp. To keep the mission secure, we soldiers were not told about what that agent was doing in your land. I only know that he was active here, we were to rendezvous with him, and then I saw Wolfram stab him."

"You're lying," accused Frank.

"No. I am saying the truth. I have told you so much so far. If I knew more about the big fire that killed all those people, why would I not tell you about this fire?"

"Because you don't want all that innocent blood on Germany's hands, that's why!" Tobin blurted.

"Constable, settle yourself!" Jack barked. But Frank could tell from Tobin's clenched teeth and shaking hands that he was only getting started.

"This is nonsense, sir. A suspicious fire happened, and we caught a German agent less than fifty kilometres away, and he don't know nothing about it? Hogwash!"

Tobin snarled at the German. "You probably lit the fire yourself!" Before he could be stopped, Tobin lunged across the table at the German and grabbed him by his shirt collar. Manfred didn't even blink as he snatched Tobin's arm and twisted it, planting the young cop face-first onto the table.

Tobin howled in agony. Frank jumped out of his chair and pulled the constable away from Manfred, though he was certain he could only do so because the German released his grip.

"Put your hands on a police officer?!" Jack yelled. "You son of a—"

"Stop, Jack!" Frank hollered. "Keep your mind on the questions and answers." He turned back to Manfred. "Why are you telling us all of this? What do you expect in return?"

"I don't want so much. I just want to get out of this war. I have had enough. I have done and felt too many things. You can lock me in a cage. Keep me there for twenty — for a hundred — years. It would not be as bad as this life."

Jack slowly leaned over the table and rested his chubby hands on its top. In a steady voice, he said, "That's one road you can take. But it doesn't have to be that way. Maybe instead of going to prison, you can stay as a free man here in Newfoundland or go to Canada? You can help the Allies win the war. You know many things about Germany, about the German Army. I know you can help us. And in exchange, you may receive leniency."

Manfred raised his eyebrows. "Leniency?"

"Mercy, I mean. If you help our side, then we will be merciful — kind — to you."

Manfred nodded knowingly. "Oh, leniency. I see now. Yes, I can give you much information. Names, missions, teach you about Germany's army. Can you … what is the word … defend me?"

"*Protect* you. We can protect you. We have made agreements with German soldiers like you before. I would need to make some calls. It takes a lot of work to make the arrangement, but if the information that you have is helpful, yes, it can be done. I think I can offer you safety and a new life." He pointed a finger at Tobin. "Make sure you put it in your notebook, constable: 'Begin procedures for ensuring safety and citizenship of German prisoner.' Get that down."

Frank thought that was a nice touch. Frank didn't know to what extent Jack's words were true. He had heard of Germans cutting deals with the Allies in exchange for lighter prison sentences, but could he and Jack actually set that for Manfred? It would have to be authorized at the highest levels — of that, he was certain. Frank studied Manfred's face. He could tell that the German was considering their words. Stirring them around in his mind. Which, Frank supposed, what Jack wanted.

Jack tapped his fingers on the tabletop. He gulped the last bit of coffee from his mug. "There is one thing I don't understand," he said. "If you Germans only wanted to set up a weather station, then why do it so close to St. John's? I mean, you could have built it on some barren stretch of coast where no one lives for twenty miles. So, why build it so close to the capital city?"

Manfred sighed heavily. Frank saw the gaps where some of his teeth had once been. He reminded Frank of a jack-o'-lantern.

"Oh, there is something big that I haven't talked with you about. I have told you what we have done in Newfoundland so far. I haven't told you what we will do next."

"What do you mean? What are your friends — I mean, the German soldiers — planning to do? You told us earlier they travelled into St. John's and left you and the other soldier to stand guard at the weather station. But we've already captured the station. So that mission is a failure."

"The mission was never to build a weather station."

Chapter 22

The men pressed through dense, evergreen foliage. They made more noise than Wolfram cared for. He was pushing them hard. He could hear the fatigue in their panting.

Speed had become more important, and so some stealth had to be sacrificed. If any villagers or an army patrol heard the Germans, they would have to deal with the problem then. Thus far, they had been lucky. There hadn't been a single patrol, or another goddamn rabbit hunter, in sight. He wondered how long luck would stay on their side. He moved faster.

Despite the cold, sweat coated his brow. He wiped it away and hoped his men didn't notice their leader was tiring. Wolfram knew he only had to keep pushing all of them at this rate for a little while longer.

Besides physical endurance, Wolfram was concerned about his men's mental stamina and how well that was holding. He knew that the mission so far had been hard, even for the most professional of soldiers. The last thing the team needed now was for its morale to collapse.

He knew he made the right choice by leaving Manfred back at their camp. How much trouble could Manfred have caused if he were with them now? With that aura of depression he seemed to emanate all the time now, Manfred would have disheartened the other men.

On the rare occasion when they stopped to rest, Wolfram would add a little humour or an optimistic line. He would smile and tell the men about the great shock they would all give to the Allies. Or, he would remind them of what was waiting for them back home. Anything to keep their spirits high. He knew that if those were going to break, now would be the time.

He could see the dimmed lights of St. John's ahead. He heard the distant voice of a yelling child over the sound of his clothes brushing against tree branches.

Wolfram found renewed strength in his thighs. His pace quickened. The moment was almost at hand. This night would see their stunning success or their dismal failure. He only needed to keep his team performing at this tempo for another few hours. Then, a short while after that, they could all be travelling away from Newfoundland. Any step away from Newfoundland was a step back to Germany.

Chapter 23

Jack stared at Manfred, "So if no weather station, why all the weather equipment, the weather charts, the code books?"

"We knew it would be a good screen for us. Your side has the advantage of reading the weather systems before us Germans. Everyone knows this. So, it would be easy to fool you that we would build a weather station in Newfoundland."

"They were all just props in some sort of bigger play?"

"Yes, a part of the deception," the German said. Despite being in his enemy's custody, Manfred smiled. Frank saw that it was the cleverness of the plot that made him proud.

"So, what is the real objective of your operation?"

"And you will get me leniency for saying this?"

"I'll make some phone calls to the highest authorities and appeal for leniency. I won't lie to you. I can't say yet what terms you will be given. But I can guarantee you that, if you do co-operate, things will be easier for you. Now, I asked you a question."

Manfred stamped his cigarette's smoldering butt into the tray. He ground it in slowly. Frank had seen this move before. It was usually followed by giving or receiving grave news — a way people mentally prepared themselves. Jack leaned over the table and waited. Finally, the German spoke.

"They plan to take control of a ship, sail it to the

harbour's entrance, and sink it. The opening is a natural choke point for water traffic. If anyone tries to stop them, soldier or citizen, they have orders to kill."

Frank heard Tobin's pencil clatter on the floor. He also heard himself exhale. The news had landed like a punch to the gut. He tried to answer, but no words came.

If a sunk ship would block the harbour's entrance, the harbour would be unusable until the wreckage was moved. That might take weeks — maybe months.

Jack must have been equally shocked, but he didn't show it. His steady stare never left Manfred's face. He drummed his fingers on the table. "Why would they target St. John's?" Jack said. "It isn't on a main shipping route like Sydney or Halifax."

"I don't know. We were only told what we needed to know to complete the mission. Sometimes, the reason for the mission is not given."

"In case you are captured."

Manfred nodded. "In case we are captured, yes."

"I see the purpose of it," Tobin said. "St. John's is by far the biggest town in Newfoundland. The harbour is the city's heart. The Germans can paralyze the entire economy of this little country, all with one sunk ship!"

Jack wearily shook his head. "Give your head a shake, constable," he said. "Impeding shipping from St. John's wouldn't make a difference to supplying Europe. Not in the big picture."

"Well, why else attack St. John's, then?" Tobin replied.

Frank's mind flashed to the warships he had seen lining the harbour only days before. "The city's crucial for launching ocean escorts, right? If St. John's Harbour gets blocked, Newfoundland doesn't have another port big enough or outfitted well enough to take over the role. The nearest port is back in maritime Canada. Plugging St. John's Harbour would throw a large monkey wrench into Allied shipping."

Frank continued, "Just think about it for a minute. The risk to the Germans is small. The most they could lose is a handful of their own soldiers, like our new friend here. But … to shut off St. John's from the Atlantic, even for a few weeks during this time in the war, would be a—."

"A damn good return on Germany's investment," Jack finished. He snorted. "A damn good step towards winning the Battle of the Atlantic. That's what that would be."

Jack, Frank, and Tobin shared glances, but none spoke. Manfred only gave a tired stare. His overcast eyes watched his audience, and Frank knew Manfred was waiting for their next play.

Jack sighed and turned to Frank. "Why don't we take a break?"

***

Outside Jack's office, Frank, Jack, and Tobin bunched together. Jack kept a close eye on Manfred through the door's window. He saw the German keeping himself occupied with a pack of cigarettes and his glass of water.

Jack leaned close to the other two men. He whispered, "Do you believe him?"

Frank responded immediately, not even having to think about the answer, "Well, he didn't put up much of a fight at that cottage, did he? I think he's telling the truth. He looks like a man who doesn't want to stay in the fight. He's just another tired soldier, ready to give up on the whole war."

Tobin blurted, "But that leads to another question! If he's playing it straight with us, then how much time do you think we have before his buddies sink a ship to the bottom of the harbour?"

Jack shrugged. "It's hard to say. I suppose men like that could march to St. John's in a day, if they really wanted. But they would want to use stealth, so that would slow them down."

Jack grabbed Tobin's shoulder and pulled him close. "We can't keep this quiet any longer. The time is too short. B'y, you wanted to tell everyone else about what's going on. Now's the moment for it. I want you to get on the phone and start alerting everyone. The rest of the constabulary, army, the navy. Call the goddamn Rockettes, if you have to. We need every man with a rifle searching that harbour *now*."

Tobin nodded. "All right," he said. "I'll alert the chief about what's going on."

"In the meantime, Frank and I will head for the harbour and catch these bastards before they set the whole goddamn place on fire."

Tobin threw his hands in the air. "Where will you start looking? That's a big harbour!"

Frank lit a cigarette. He again pictured the harbour as he had seen it first-hand. He saw the castle tower sitting on top of Signal Hill, the fleet of naval vessels lining the harbour, the harbour's entrance, and men rushing about their business.

Then he thought about The Battery — that out-of-time village at the base of Signal Hill. He remembered its fishing shacks, slipways, and rickety piers that looked ready to tumble into the sea, and he was reminded of the photos they found at Kelly's house. Frank spoke without meaning to. "Why did the Germans want photos of The Battery?" He understood it to be a place without military facilities, a place that didn't matter.

Frank caught his breath. *How had I missed it?* For all of his study and sifting through the clues, he was stunned that he hadn't seen it before.

Frank clutched Jack's shoulder and pulled forcefully enough to spin his partner until they stood square.

"The Battery! Don't you see?" Frank exclaimed. "It's not about what's there. It's about what's not there — security. There's hardly anything of military value over there, right? You got that army supply dock, but that's not covering the whole waterfront, right?"

"Yeah, that's right," Jack said. There's a big stretch of land, between the army dock and one of the Canadian gun sites. The Battery is almost completely free of military. It's just a bunch of fishing wharves and a few houses. You can get there by taking a road that runs through the army dock, or by taking another road that runs up through the land just above it."

"So, how much security do you think is over there?"

Jack ran his hands through his hair. "The supply dock doesn't have any guards on it, as far as I know. And that dock is pretty quiet at this time of night. The Americans rely on one Canadian guard in a little wooden booth. He watches one of the roads running through the dock."

"Where are you going with this, sir?" Tobin asked.

Jack took a deep breath and stared at the puzzled expression on Tobin's face. Why the hell wasn't Tobin catching on yet? When he spoke again, it was in a calmer tone. "If there isn't much guarding over there, then that's where the Germans will try to penetrate the harbour!"

"You're right!" Frank said. His eyes bulged. "Let's hope there isn't a ship at that dock big enough for them to use." Jack nodded, as if he needed to give another affirmation. "All right. Battery, here we come. Frank, pray you're right about this. We won't get any other chances."

Frank wasn't sure he was right, but it was the best hunch anybody had.

Frank knew that the face-off ahead wouldn't be simple. But he also saw it for what it was — a chance to foil a Nazi operation and an opportunity to strike back a blow in his brother's name.

He took a deep draw from his cigarette and let the smoke burn his lungs slightly before he exhaled. He gave Jack a stern look. "Let me get my coat."

Jack beamed. "All right, but I'm driving!"

Chapter 24

Beth was clearing money out of the store's register. She tried to keep her mind focused on the task at hand, but her thoughts kept turning to Frank.

She sighed. It was just as well that things hadn't gone further with him. Between her volunteer work with the Red Cross and the long days at her husband's store, she had little time for romance.

She was lucky to have gotten out of the relationship with Frank — if it could even be called that — as safely as she had. She was fine, apart from some small bruises earned in the alley fight, and some awkward questions from the Red Cross's Assistant Commissioner.

The questions had obviously been well answered, though — and her supervisor didn't know anything about her brief time as a citizen detective — since she'd been allowed to use the Red Cross car again. Beth had said she needed to pick up more supplies that night from the warehouse in The Battery, and the keys were given without hesitation.

She glumly placed what little cash the store had made that day into an envelope. It wasn't much, and even so, none of it was hers. Her husband had instructed her to leave it under the store's counter, and he would pick it up in the morning. "Every coin!"

Beth's taste of excitement during her brief stint as a sleuth made returning to her mundane life difficult. She was having a hard time being optimistic about her future. Before the month was finished, her brother would probably have her situated in that little affordable house on Gower Street that he mentioned. The idea of living alone did not appeal to her.

A thunderous bang shattered the night's silence. She dropped to her knees in fear, and clung to the bottom of the counter. The movement sent a bolt of pain through her back. Her jaws locked. She cursed through clenched teeth. It took two tries before she finally clambered to her feet. She heard the windows in the back of the store rattling in their frames.

The echo faded. Beth had seen enough war footage at the cinema to recognize that there had been an explosion. Her concern was what had blown up and if anyone was hurt — *God forbid.*

She rushed outside of the shop and found dozens of pedestrians frozen in place. Their faces, bathed in an orange light, were turned towards the west. She moved to get a better view, stepping off the sidewalk and into the middle of the street. She was not worried she'd be struck. All the vehicles had halted, and their drivers and passengers were scrambling out to see what was happening.

A fireball had formed in the sky at the downtown's western edge. Beth saw giant fingers of flame reaching fifty feet above the rooftops. The blast had been deafening, but now the only sound heard in downtown St. John's was the inferno's crackle.

Then, at least thirty flares were simultaneously fired into the sapphire night sky. The armies and navies had responded by setting the sky alight. Any part of the downtown not already illuminated by the fire was now cast in the flares' glow. The moving yellow light rolled into the city's shadows, revealing what hid within them.

A second, slightly quieter explosion erupted where the first had been. Many of the people around Beth flinched, and the collective trance broke. Some started running in the opposite direction.

The man who owned a restaurant adjacent to her store yelled, "Beth, go on. Get out of here. Run on back home!"

"What's going on?" she cried.

The owner wiped his sweating brow with his stained apron. "I don't know. It's like that goddamn hostel fire all over again. We need to get out of here!"

A young man standing in the doorway of the restaurant yelled, "No, we need to help. That explosion was over at the train station. I'd bet my life on that. There's got to be people hurt. We need to help them!"

"We need to save ourselves, is what we need to do!" the restaurant owner said.

In disbelief, the young man dropped his clean-shaven, square jaw. He replied, "B'y, I'm never eating at your restaurant again!" and ran towards the explosion.

Beth knew what she had to do. Mention of the hostel fire made her think of her brother and Frank. Perhaps they were involved in whatever was happening in the harbour. She limped back to the hardware store.

She wasn't the only one fleeing. Other people were now moving away from the waterfront. Like salmon swimming upstream, they raced up the downtown's steep streets. Some moved at a brisk walk, while others dodged through the crowd at a full run.

Beth busted in through the store's door and snatched the car keys from the countertop. She was still going to drive to The Battery, as she had planned for the night, to retrieve supplies and bring them to the Red Cross hostel.

The hostel would be busy tonight with the many wounded — and their families — who would need friendly hands to care for them.

First, she needed to call her brother's office and know that he was safe. She dialled his phone number and prayed to God that he answered.

Chapter 25

The lights from the harbour pierced the otherwise dark night and illuminated the freighter moored at the dock two hundred feet away.

They didn't know which ship to target prior to arriving at the harbour — Wolfram knew this was one of the plan's weakest points. Because the ship's arrival and departure times were kept top secret, they couldn't choose a ship to overtake prior to reaching the harbour. Plus, the Allies frequently changed the times at the last moment to mislead German intelligence. His team had to take their chances finding a suitable ship once they were on site.

The men who'd planned the operation back in Germany had been confident that a sizeable freighter would be present, and they were right. The freighter Wolfram saw moored at the dock in front of him was a formidable ship. That it managed to fit through the harbour's small opening was a surprise. He knew that a ship that size sitting on the bottom of the harbour, blocking that narrow entrance, would be an enormous blow for the Allied war effort.

He lowered his binoculars and scanned the docks again for any sign that he had been detected. None. The lone guard he had seen had passed by two minutes ago. The guard didn't show the slightest concern for the tool shed he and his men were occupying. If he had looked, he would have noticed the broken lock and the operation might have ended there. As luck — or God — would have it, he didn't.

Wolfram stepped away from the tool shed's tiny window. He turned to his men who were crammed in behind him. The cabin they were using as a camp was a luxurious hotel compared to their current shelter, but at least they weren't outside.

He assessed his team. The men shivered and huffed. Some could clearly use an extra night of sleep. All were relieved to finally take a break. The speed of their journey had taken its toll. It may have been the increasing cold that had spurred them on, but whatever it was, they had reached the city faster than expected. Wolfram was grateful to see that some things were going in their favour.

He patted one man on the shoulder and felt him shake under his damp coat. The man reeked of the woods — *like pine needles*, Wolfram thought. All the men must smell that way, he figured — himself included.

None of the men complained. No one suggested that they stop. Though his men had been made uncomfortable and were tired, they had never been close to quitting either and neither had Wolfram. He had to see it through. All his work, his losses, *Germany's* losses, couldn't be for nothing.

In the distance, he heard a thunderous bang. The men flinched. The bomb they had planted at the train station had exploded on time. Soon the harbour would lock down. Not a mouse would be able to crawl. But for the next brief while, all eyes in the city would be turned towards that burning train station. This was their chance to execute the next phase of the operation.

"Courage, men. This will be over soon enough. I know that Captain Baumbach has a bottle of the best whiskey back on board. He told me that he got it from one of those little Scotch islands where they make the best of the best. He said those Scots usually keep it for themselves and don't sell it to foreigners. But he got his hands on a full flask of it. He said that he has saved it for a special occasion. He told me that when we return from our mission, he'll have it waiting for us. A nice drink of Scotch would be welcome right now, hey? To warm the bones?"

In the dim light, he could still see a couple of his men smile. Wolfram smiled back. He was glad to see that at least one or two people believed his lie — or pretended to. How many of them would even make it off this island, let alone have prime whiskey waiting for them?

"We cannot stay here for long, so I will say this fast. It is time for you all to know the complete details of our mission, so you may each perform your part towards its success. You all know that we will be sinking a ship in the harbour in order to disrupt Allied operations. As the English would say, *Easier said than done*." Wolfram forced himself to smile, but this time, none of the men returned his smile.

He continued, "To ensure the ship sinks when and where needed, simply placing charges with timers onto the ship's hull would be too risky. We need to infiltrate a freighter, capture the captain and crew, and force them to sail the ship into the entrance. Once there, we will steal their clothes, sabotage the ship's engines, drop anchor, and lock the crew into a room. The ship will not be going anywhere after that. Then we will set our charges against the insides of the ship's hull. Just below the waterline. We will set the timers on the charges to give us enough time to escape. A short row in one of the ship's lifeboats will bring us to the harbour's south end, which has fewer guards and civilians.

"But we will be spotted leaving the ship," one of the men said. "What happens when someone stops us? They will bring the sailors of every Allied navy down on our heads."

Wolfram replied, "I don't think anyone will stop us. We will have escaped and be running back to our forest camp before the explosions. And if anyone sees us, then what *will* they see? They will see a captain and a handful of his crewmen rowing for the docks — no different than all the other small boats rowing back and forth from the big ships to land. People will probably think we left some important business back on shore. Or maybe that we want to have one last drink at a favourite tavern before we sail for Europe."

He worried that he was embellishing too much. A good commanding officer understood that, despite orders and military discipline, there was always a little salesmanship involved. In the darkness, Wolfram tried to read his men's faces. Did they believe him?

"A captain and his crew?" One man asked.

"Yes, by the time we leave the ship, we will be disguised in the clothes of the captain and crew. Trust me, at that point, they won't ever need them again."

Wolfram saw the soldier take a breath and knew that the man had caught Wolfram's meaning.

"We'll be back in the forest by the time the charges detonate. At that point, everyone will be too focused on the burning ship in the harbour to stop us. It will hardly matter. I expect that a few holes blown in the bottom of even a big ship will sink it in minutes."

"What then?"

"Once we travel back to the coastline where we landed, we will fire a flare to signal the same U-boat that delivered us there. It will retrieve us, and then our mission is complete. Men … my brothers, the blow that we strike tonight is a blow for the Fatherland."

Chapter 26

The Studebaker raced down the hill. Jack wrestled the wheel to keep the car from crashing into vehicles and terrified pedestrians. A near miss with an elderly woman sent the car riding up onto the sidewalk. Jack pulled the wheel to his left. The tires screamed against the pavement. They hit a bump that sent the Studebaker soaring. Frank, who was riding in the passenger seat, catapulted upwards. His head hit the car's roof, and he flopped back into his seat.

"You got me seeing stars now, you bloody madman! Slow down!" Frank yelled.

"We won't catch them if we slow down," Jack hollered.

"We won't catch them if we're dead either!"

Frank was about to protest further when a loud bang halted him. He looked through the car's rear window and saw flames licking at the sky from at least a mile away. He could see flames above the rooftops and knew the blaze must be big. A volley of flares was sent skywards, lighting the city's distant downtown area.

"Something over west just blew!" he hollered.

Jack didn't take his eyes off the road to look at either Frank or the fire. "Yeah, I heard!" he said. "I don't know what it was, and we're not going to find out either!"

"Are you mad? That could be the Germans right there!"

"No, that's just their distraction. If they really want to go to The Battery, over northeast, why not do something to draw everyone's attention away from it?"

"I hope you're right, Jack. Step on it!"

They reached one of The Battery's twisting dirt roads. Its potholes jolted Frank from his seat, and he slammed against the passenger side door. He was about to curse at Jack again, when he noticed that the road ahead had almost completely disappeared. They had hit a thick wall of fog. Normally, Frank liked the fog. There was something about it that made the world feel smaller and more intimate. But now, he was concerned that it might be the leading cause of his death.

"Slow down! You're going to kill me before the damned Germans get a chance!"

But Jack was merciless. Their car bounded past The Battery's boat slips, fishing shacks, and modest homes. Frank thought they were about to collide with a stack of lumber, when Jack hit the brakes. He parked in the middle of the street. The area was deserted. Frank examined their surroundings and couldn't see anything noteworthy.

"Why'd you stop?" Frank asked. "Where's the army dock?"

"It's still a few hundred yards from here, but we don't want to park too close to it. The Germans will look for anything suspicious, and a blind man at the other end of the harbour would be able to spot a speeding Studebaker. From here on, we'll walk. But first things first."

Jack reached into the back seat and pulled up a shotgun that Frank had seen him take from his office's gun rack. Its chrome barrel and tubular magazine shone like polished coins. Jack removed a half box of shells from the glove compartment and pounded them into the magazine.

"I just got this new pump-action." Jack said. "Never really had the chance to use it yet. I brought it for myself, but … I'd rather you have it," Jack said. He handed it stock first to Frank.

Frank knew that what Jack was really handing him was the best chance at survival for either of them. He was moved, but now wasn't the time for sentimentality. Instead, Frank nodded his thanks and hoped that was enough.

"Before we go out there, you better take some extra firepower yourself. I have my .38 to fall back on, so you can take this," Frank said. He reached into his coat pocket and handed a pistol to Jack. "I took that off Manfred. He was carrying it when we arrested him." Frank said. "That's a Colt .45. It has a seven-round magazine."

"That's a fine gun right there, Frank." Jack said. He expertly turned the Colt over in his hands, giving the sleek pistol an inspection before ejecting its magazine, and then putting it back into place. He was clearly satisfied that the gun was loaded and in good working condition. Jack placed it in his own coat.

"You already know how to handle one of those?" Frank said with surprise.

"I have one at home just like it. Brought it back from France after the war."

They exited the car and strode towards the dock. They travelled only two hundred feet before stopping. Sandwiched between a fisherman's storehouse and some overturned rowboats was the Canadian Army's sentry box. It was the size and shape of a phone booth — big enough to allow for a single guard. It was a miserable place to wait out a watch shift, Frank was sure. Its wooden planks looked waterlogged. Given the city's inclement weather, Frank doubted they were ever dry.

The sentry box had no door. As they approached, Frank was surprised to see no one standing inside the post. He concluded that the single Canadian soldier who was supposed to be manning it must be busy making his rounds.

"There's supposed to be a security guard here, but where in the hell he got to, I can't tell," Jack said. "Maybe the Germans found him first."

Frank couldn't tell if Jack was joking, but his comment still made Frank's finger tighten on the trigger.

"Damn, that's a problem," Jack said. "I was hoping that he could help even the odds." Their chances against crack German soldiers were dismal.

After a short walk, Frank saw the army dock lying less than a hundred feet ahead of him. A lone lamppost flickered at the dock's entrance. Frank wished that there had been more lights installed (and in working order). The docked vessels lent some light, but these were blurred by the blanket of fog that shrouded the harbour. Frank muttered a curse. In their haste, they had forgotten to bring a flashlight.

Frank took in a few of the dock's other features. It was little more than a giant concrete rectangle, with a large, central building. Frank guessed the building was for administration and sheltered storage. Loads of crates and building materials were scattered across the dock. Two cranes and a collection of small tractors and trailers added to the clutter.

Frank leaned against a heap of metal pipes and listened closely. He heard nothing but his partner's footsteps on concrete and the whine of far-off alarms. He surveyed their surroundings and didn't spot a single citizen, soldier, or suspect. He also confirmed something else — the army dock was poorly defended. Apart from a gate that had been left unlocked, Frank saw no security measures taken. Jack had been right — the US army was counting on the lone Canadian guard for surveillance. Frank supposed the Americans believed the greatest threats would come by sea, and so the harbour's guns and warships would provide protection. They hadn't counted on a threat by land.

"So, how do you want to do this?" Jack asked.

"We split up. You head in that direction along the waterfront. I'll go the other way."

"I don't like the sound of that."

"Me either, but it's the only way we're going to find them in time."

He hoped his words didn't sound as hollow as they felt in his heart. He knew the chance of locating the Germans was slim and he knew their luck had to run out some time.

In unison, the men turned to the sound of an approaching vehicle. Frank's police instincts told him to note the make and model. However, he could only see the headlights shining like twin lighthouses through the fog.

Frank stepped towards the vehicle and raised his shotgun to his chest, not quite shouldering it. The vehicle stopped near Jack's Studebaker. A figure exited and walked towards them. Frank was about to issue a warning when Jack snarled, "Christ, it's that idiot, Toby. What's he doing here?"

Upon hearing that, Frank finally recognized the figure as Tobin. He breathed out his relief. Another man would help balance the odds if they did find the Germans. Perhaps they would now have a chance.

Jack stomped towards Tobin. "Constable!" Jack said. "What in the devil are you doing here? Did I not tell you to stay at the goddamn station?"

"I told everyone what's going on, and you can hear the alarms sounding, right? There's nothing more for me to do at the station that can't be done by someone else."

"That's beside the point. I—"

"Oh, kiss my arse, Fowler. I'm here now, and I'm staying. You may outrank me, but I'm a Newfoundlander too, and I have as much of a right to fight for the goddamn island as you do." He reached under his greatcoat and pulled out his .38 revolver.

Jack balked. Frank smiled.

"Good for you, constable," Frank said and patted Tobin on the shoulder. "Good for you."

Jack regained his composure and said, "All right then. You brought along a flashlight, at least. That's more than me or Frank did. So come on."

Tobin nodded at Jack, and asked "So what's the plan?"

"Look for anything suspicious, constable. In particular, check around for any ship that's big enough to plug the harbour's Narrows."

"You mean like those?" Tobin said as he pointed past Frank's shoulder.

Frank turned. Through the mist, he saw three great, dark shapes moored against the dock. He approached and recognized them as a Coast Guard ship and a pair of freighters. Frank guessed that the first vessel, which was the one closest to them, was too small. Yet the other two would serve the Nazis' purpose.

"Yeah let's check those. Forget about the first one, though. Too little," he said.

Chapter 27

The three men walked towards the freighter. Jack shone his flashlight along the length of the hull. The men craned their necks to get a better look at the ship's features in the dim light. Frank gave an occasional glance at the surrounding area. This did little good due to the tight cloak of mist draped across the dock. He shuddered and hoped that, whoever may be hidden in the fog's folds were as blind to him as he was to them.

There wasn't much else to examine, apart from a utility shed, a few parked vehicles, and what Frank believed was some sort of refuelling station. He searched the dock for movement and saw none. All was stationary and inanimate — coils of rope, a fuel can, a misplaced toolbox that they would be lucky not to trip over before the night was finished.

Frank searched the deck of the freighter for any person he could question. But again, there wasn't a sailor in sight.

The constable waved his flashlight's beam across coils of rope and said, "I don't see anything out of place. There's nobody here. We can check on that shed over there, but I'm pretty certain—"

"How can you tell in this shit light and thick fog?" Jack replied. "Hitler could have hidden a fucking panzer division over here, and how would we see it?"

"You're right. We need more light," Frank said.

He aimed his shotgun skywards and fired three rounds. He hoped that a shotgun's roar would bring the reaction that they needed. Jack realized what Frank was trying to accomplish and copied him. He blazed his Colt upwards. The echoes of gunfire faded. Frank held his breath. He looked to Jack and saw that his partner was doing the same.

More flares filled the sky directly over them, casting their yellow light across the whole dock. Frank smiled. Everyone in St. John's would be looking their way now and their flares would light up the dock like a theatre's stage.

In the flares' flickering light, Frank saw what he had simultaneously hoped and feared he would see — less than a hundred feet ahead of him was a group of figures moving through the fog. He could only catch glimpses of them, but that was enough to give him an indication of what he was seeing — five armed men. These wraithlike figures were soundless, letting the fog envelope them as they moved down the dock. A few more steps and they would vanish.

"There! There they are!" Frank cried.

Jack pivoted to see the men. He dashed down the dock, faster than Frank would have expected for a man his size.

He pulled his badge from his coat and yelled, "Newfoundland Constabulary! Stop what you're—." It was all that he had time to say before one of the Germans yelled a command. Frank didn't need to speak German to know what the command meant.

The rest of the Germans raised their weapons and let loose a thunderstorm from the mouths of their submachine guns. The gunfire hacked through the harbour's silence. Frank heard the *pang-pang* of their rounds striking the metal refuelling station to his left. A chunk of concrete blew free from the dock and stung his hand. But these were stray rounds. It was Jack who had drawn their attention. This gave Frank and Tobin the precious second needed to duck behind the refuelling station. For the second time that night, Frank was diving for cover from automatic fire.

Jack returned fire, all the while crouching and sidestepping. Frank saw one, maybe two of the operatives fall. Jack was either a hell of a better marksman than Frank thought, or he was getting damned lucky.

Jack tried to make himself a difficult target, but it didn't matter. He managed to run through most of his pistol's magazine before German bullets found him. He howled and collapsed.

Frank pulled Tobin close and yelled "Jack's down! We need to get him. He's as good as dead over there!"

"Yes, sir!" was all Tobin said. Frank couldn't have guessed what was about to happen.

Tobin charged from behind the station and sprinted down the dock to their wounded colleague. The Germans paused for a moment, holding their fire. Perhaps they were in as much awe of the constable's bravery as Frank was. Jack could only writhe in pain, making Tobin's task of loading him onto his shoulders more difficult. The Germans resumed fire. Frank was certain that both of his friends would get cut down before they reached safety.

The same German who had given the command to open fire lunged to retrieve a satchel that had fallen to the dock. While he fumbled with the satchel's contents, he barked at his one remaining comrade and pointed towards Tobin and Jack. Frank didn't need to see his dog tag to know that the German who had given the command was Captain Wolfram himself.

The commanded soldier charged towards Tobin and Jack. Frank was certain that neither man was aware of the German bearing down on them. What Wolfram had commanded for his man to do was a mystery. Whether the German was intending to kill or capture them, there was no way and no time to determine. Frank had to assume the worst.

Frank shouldered his 12-gauge and sighted in on the German. He didn't aim at the man, though. If he had, by the time he pulled the trigger, the German would have moved, and Frank would have missed. Instead, he aimed ahead of the German and swung his gun at the same pace as the man was running, to maintain his lead. When his aim was steady, he pulled the trigger. The shotgun roared out its load. A tight pattern of buckshot peppered across a six-inch space on the man's chest. The German was sent sprawling. It was a good shot that filled Frank with hope. A few more like that and they might just win this night after all.

Meanwhile Tobin had managed to carry Jack fireman-style back to the refuelling station. That Jack outweighed the constable by forty pounds was not overlooked by Frank. Nor was it unnoticed that the German gunfire had ceased.

Frank aimed at Wolfram, who had his hands in the satchel and fumbled with its contents. It should have been an easy shot. However, Wolfram removed his hands from the inside, and with a two-handed toss, sent the satchel hurtling towards Frank. The satchel burst in mid-air.

Frank's ears popped. A white light exploded against his eyes while the hand of an invisible giant slapped him. His entire body lifted from the dock and flew past its edge. He had a split second to twist himself and brace for the waters below. He hit the water headfirst.

***

Beth heard the whine of sirens in the distance, as she carefully drove the Red Cross ambulance through one of

The Battery's winding roads. She searched the shadows and drifting fog for anyone else. She worried she would hit someone, but there was luckily no one else. There was no one. That explosion must have either sent people into hiding or drawn away anyone who would otherwise have been there. Even the guardsman — the one she was accustomed to seeing at this time of night — wasn't at his sentry box. All the commotion must have had him doing an extra set of rounds.

Beth was shaken — she hadn't been able to reach Jack after the explosion. She knew his business must be urgent, but she needed to know he was safe.

She was surprised to see the outlines of two cars, barely visible through the fog. They were parked near the army dock's entrance. It was unusual to see other cars parked at this time of the evening.

It occurred to her that the cars could belong to German spies or their allies. She shook her head — that was an absurd idea, a product of rattled nerves.

"That's madness," she muttered. "The Germans aren't at the bloody dock." She stopped her Red Cross vehicle next to the two cars.

One of them was much like her brother's Studebaker. Could it be Jack was at the dock too? After all, how many cars like his Studebaker were there in St. John's?

Ahead, she heard the low murmur of voices. She cursed the night and fog for hiding the speakers. She opened her mouth to call to them, and the thought of Germans flooded back to her. She dismissed it as a preposterous idea fuelled by her paranoia. The unseen owners of those voices were probably servicemen working a late-night shift. Any moment, a break in the fog would let her see them plainly.

She heard Jack's voice. What he said, she missed, but she knew it was him. Then gunfire cracked the night wide open.

Someone ahead of her was shooting. The repetitive bursting forced her to cover her ears. Someone ahead of her was waging a war on the army dock.

She felt a rush of air as something flew past her cheek. She realized it had been a bullet. A second gust of air brushed her nose.

Beth's muscles locked for a second. She retreated backwards two steps. The sudden movement caught her back's muscles unready. Ripples of pain ran along her body. The agony forced her to her knees. She gritted her teeth and tried to raise herself. Her body wasn't prepared to obey.

A ball of light lit the greyness ahead of her. A thunderous roar filled her covered ears. Even at a distance, she felt the invisible power of the explosion.

The blast displaced some of the fog. It also provided enough light by which to see. She saw two men hiding behind some sort of structure. One was writhing. Somehow, she knew it was Jack.

She didn't want to watch the unfolding action. She wanted to flee the danger before it found her. But Jack was hurt, and he needed his sister.

Beth forced herself off the ground and rushed over to her brother.

***

Cold crashed against Frank as he shot into the blackness. A lung full of water forced his body to convulse. He pawed for the surface, realized he was swimming downwards, and then righted himself. He didn't know how deep he had sunk, but he prayed that he would break free soon.

His lungs were crying for air once he finally emerged. He coughed, gasped, and flailed. God, he had never been so cold in his life.

Frank had never been a good swimmer, but he managed to dog-paddle the twenty feet or so to the dock. With each short stroke, he coughed up more sea water. He climbed up one of the large truck tires hanging over the dock's side. That was harder than he thought it would be. There was a ringing in his ears. His balance was distorted. He wasn't sure if these side effects were caused by the explosion or a result of being submerged. Once he'd reached the top of the dock, his hands were already starting to lose sensation.

The remains of the exploded satchel lay burning in the middle of the dock. By its firelight, Frank could see the explosion had burned or blown away the fog in the immediate area. Spiralling vapours bordering that space were now rolling back to reconquer their territory. He reached into his coat pocket and removed his service revolver. He pointed the .38 from side to side, searching the dock for Germans.

He saw Tobin and Jack sheltered near the refuelling station. To his surprise, Beth was with them. How or why she was at the dock, he didn't know. He could get the answers later. Frank rushed over to them.

Jack looked to be doing better than expected, for someone who had been shot. He was still conscious, and that was something. Beth was kneeling next to him.

She removed her thin scarf and placed it over his hip. Beth put Jack's left hand on top of the scarf and said, "Apply pressure, Jack. That will help control the bleeding." She then removed her wool shawl and placed it over his chest. "We need to keep you warm."

Frank tapped Tobin on the shoulder and said, "I'm back, Toby!"

"Frank!" the constable cried. "Thank God you're alive! I thought that bomb had blown a thousand pieces of you into the water."

"It damn near did," Frank answered. "How's Jack doing?"

"Best I can tell, a bullet grazed him here in the left hip. Another bullet hit him in the wrist. The hip isn't my big worry right now. He only got nicked, and the bleeding is rather minor. I'm more worried about the wrist."

As if to emphasize his point, a geyser of blood shot out of Jack's right wrist.

"Christ, he'll bleed to death if we don't get him to a hospital fast," Frank said.

Beth reached across and snatched Frank's belt. She expertly unbuckled it and slipped it off his waist. With what were clearly practised hands, she put a tourniquet on Jack's upper right arm. "There, that will slow the flow," she said. Beth removed one of Jack's own gloves and used it to cover the bleeding wrist. She pressed too hard. Jack yelped.

Frank saw that Jack's hand hung lifelessly below his wound. Frank took that flopping hand in his own and said, "Jack I want you to squeeze my hand as hard as you can. Can you do that, sport?" Frank could tell from the expression on Jack's face that his partner was trying to comply, but Frank felt nothing. Frank wondered if Jack would ever use that hand again.

Frank squeezed Jack's hand and said, "Don't worry, Jack. I'm not going anywhere. I'll stay right here with you until help comes."

Jack exploded to life and shook violently. "What? The hell you will! You're going after those bastards, and you're going to tear a strip off them! That's what you're going to do!"

Maybe it was Frank's surprise at the outburst that made Jack settle, but in a calmer voice, Jack continued. "Frank, if you want to help me, go break those bastards. Toby and Beth can handle the nursing from here. They've managed to come through on everything else lately."

Jack removed his bloodied hand from his injured hip and tugged Tobin's coat sleeve. "Thanks, buddy. I mean that," Jack said.

Tobin gingerly moved Jack's hand away and placed it back on the hip. "I know you do, sir," Tobin said. "But for now, just keep quiet. You know — as much as you're able, anyhow. Save your strength."

Tobin looked to Frank and said, "He's right, though. We can take care of him until help arrives. It shouldn't be too long now. Look over across the water."

By flare light, Frank could see dozens of men swarming across the waterfront, like army ants who just had their hill kicked. Soon they would arrive at the army dock. *Jack will have all the care he needs then*, Frank told himself and prayed that he was right.

He looked down the long stretch of dock, as far as the fog would allow, before it turned into a wall of grey. "How many of them do you think are left?" Frank said.

"Just the one." Tobin said. "The guy who tossed the bomb. I saw him slip away down the dock. Clever bastard. The bomb was a diversion, wasn't it, Frank? Like a squid shooting its ink, so it can blind you and buy some time to escape."

"Yeah, that's what it was all right." Frank wondered if Wolfram was still there hiding, or if he'd already escaped. Frank didn't believe there would be many cards left to play in what he knew was the last hand. Now that everyone else was dead or otherwise dispatched, what else was left but for Wolfram and him to meet?

"All right then. You two just try to treat him until help comes. I'm going after that bastard."

"Whip his arse!" Beth cried.

"If you're going alone, then take this," Tobin said and handed Frank one of the Germans' submachine guns that lay next to him. Thank God. Even while caring for Jack, Tobin had had the presence of mind to grab some of the heavy firepower that lay strewn about the dock.

Frank looked into Jack's eyes. He wanted to say so much, but all that came out was, "Good luck." He didn't wait for a response before he strode away, surrendering what he knew may be the last glimpse anyone would ever get of him to the harbour's swirling mists.

Chapter 28

Wolfram replaced the magazine of his submachine gun and chambered a round. He knew he didn't have much ammunition left. Most of it was lost in the skirmish. He had fled from the dock and raced along the harbourfront until he had finally taken cover in a nearby construction site. He lay behind a bulldozer and considered his next move.

Wolfram peered from behind his cover. All he saw was more heavy machinery and some piles of sheet metal. The ground was pockmarked with muddy holes that reminded him of the landscapes he'd encountered during the Great War. Some holes were large enough to hide in, but Wolfram knew that deep pools of muddy water lay at their bottoms. On the harbour's opposite side, he saw the flashing lights sparkling across the city's downtown.

He pulled up his pant leg and examined his wound. It was difficult to see, but even without light, he knew it was bad. Blood had already soaked into his sock. He pulled an emergency medical kit from his coat pocket and searched for a bandage of appropriate size. He covered the wound and applied pressure. He cursed himself. If only he hadn't ordered Manfred to stay at the camp. The team's medic would be the best person to treat him. But he didn't have time for regrets, not with those men approaching. How many enemies had there been? Three, at least.

After strapping his belt around his leg, he gently moved the leg to test its mobility. The pain was enough to make him cry aloud. Still, he was relieved that he could move it. He took it as a sign that nothing was broken.

There was no way he'd be able to make it back to the base camp. Even with the night and fog screening him, reaching Conception Bay couldn't be done. In an hour, the backwoods would be teeming with search parties and their scent-hunting dogs. In his bloody condition, they would smell him out instantly.

But maybe the means of escape lay in his enemies themselves. If he finished them, he could don their clothes, steal their car, and drive away. It wasn't a seamless plan, but he didn't have time to think of anything better.

He shifted his weight to his good leg and held onto the side of the bulldozer for support. He slowly pulled himself off the ground. He was almost standing upright when the pain in his left leg overpowered him. Again, he howled. He would have fallen into the mud if he had not been holding the bulldozer.

He lowered himself back down. He reached into his pocket and removed a pack of cigarettes and a lighter. It hurt to do so, but that wasn't about to stop him. If the end was upon him, he would go down fighting and have the comfort of a final cigarette.

He lit it and inhaled deeply. He knew the cigarette wasn't anaesthetic, but it gave him some relief. Holding the strong smoke in his lungs, Wolfram closed his eyes and reflected on all that had been lost up to that point, all that had been sacrificed. His men and the people they had killed — were they all for nothing? And now he was about to lose his own life knowing it wouldn't be enough to help tip the scales in favour of the Fatherland. And as grim a conclusion as that was to reach, he had no answer to his question, except another question: What else was there left to do?

The sound of approaching footsteps broke his concentration. He finally exhaled and watched the smoke mingle with the fog. *Strike fast. Speed is the killer.* That was the message he always preached to his men. But they were all gone now, and he would likely be joining them soon. Wolfram gritted his teeth and pulled himself upwards again. He stepped away from the bulldozer and shuffled towards the sound of his coming enemies. *Strike fast.*

***

Frank felt the cold bite his fingers. He balled up those on his free hand, brought his hand near his mouth, and breathed merciful, warm air onto his numb digits. Those on his gun hand would have to wait. He could barely keep the submachine gun steady. Soon, he wouldn't be able to operate it at all. He needed to beat Wolfram before his hands froze completely.

He reached the opposite end of the dock. Through the fog, a metal tool shed materialized, and Frank realized Wolfram may not have travelled as far as he had thought. Perhaps he was lying in ambush, waiting for his overconfident pursuers.

Frank crouched and stalked his way towards the shed. He hoped that his footsteps didn't sound as loud to anyone inside the shed as they did to him. He reached for the door and felt a loose chain hanging near the handle. The chain's rattle was loud — too loud. Frank bit his lip.

He swung the door open and expected to see the silhouette of his enemy shifting about in the shed's shadows. He almost fired off a shot, but his training kept him in check.

There was a person on the shed's floor. Could they have gotten lucky and already struck Wolfram with a killing blow? Frank knelt to one knee. He landed in a warm puddle. He struck his Zippo repeatedly before it lit. When it finally did, he saw the blood and he knew the person was dead.

The corpse wore a military uniform. The throat had been slashed open. No, not slashed, torn — like an animal's jaws had closed upon it and shook it open. Frank was certain that the guard's death was quick, at least.

Frank remembered Jack's comment from earlier, about the Germans possibly reaching the security guard first, and he trembled. If only they had arrived a few minutes earlier, this man would still be going home to his family tonight.

He left the shed and resumed his trek until he reached the end of the dock. There were two options available. To his right, he could follow a narrow laneway that led between a cluster of homes, or to his left, he could search a construction site. Given the growing vigilance and panic along the harbourfront, he doubted Wolfram would head towards the homes. Frank chose the second option.

Frank had barely walked five paces into the site when he smelled it. The staunch odour of French cigarettes filled his nose. Its pungency was unmistakeable. His mind flashed to when he killed the German in the forest earlier that evening.

Frank's heart froze. His breathing stopped. He searched the darkness for any sign of Wolfram, but he saw none. He heard the scrape of boots in the mud and knew that Wolfram was approaching. He couldn't find him.

He has me, Frank thought. He's here someplace. I can't see him, but he can see me. He can see me. Any second, he's going to put a bullet through me. Or he's going to rip out my throat like he did to that guy in the shed. He's got me. I'm—

Then Frank did see him. At first, it was just a hint of a man — part of a form moving in veils of fog and hazy flare light. If Frank hadn't been searching so intently to find his adversary, he could have passed unnoticed. He didn't see his enemy's face, but he saw that burning cigarette dangling from one hand. He could only assume that the other held something far more lethal.

With each step, the featureless shape resolved itself. And with each step, the gap closed between them. Frank didn't wait for the form in front of him to finally take its full shape. He didn't even take time to aim properly. His training had taught him that at this close a range, marksmanship hardly mattered. It was all about who could put the most lead into the air the fastest. He socked his submachine gun to his waist, pulled the trigger, and held the bucking weapon as best as his numbing hands would let him.

The automatic fire added welcome muzzle flashes to the dimness. They illuminated Wolfram like dozens of cameras lighting up a movie star. Frank caught Wolfram in microsecond flickers. An open mouth. A twisted grimace. A falling body. By the time Frank's gun had emptied, Wolfram lay in a puddle. Frank thought for certain Wolfram was dead. But he could still hear gurgling from Wolfram's mouth, see one of his arms move. Wolfram made no effort to either attack or defend himself. He only grabbed his chest and tried to raise himself from the muddy water.

Still, Frank knew that the German hadn't released his own weapon. It still lay loosely clutched in his hand, fingers not far from the trigger. Knowing that his own submachine gun had spent its last round, Frank cast it aside. Frank drew his revolver and stepped close enough that he could see the blood running between Wolfram's fingers.

"I know you bastards can speak English. The game's over, Wolfram. You lost. Drop your weapon. Do it. Now!"

Wolfram breathed two large gulps of air. Each time, the gurgling became louder. He finally made his move.

Wolfram raised his gun from the mud and placed it under his chin. Before Frank could speak, Wolfram had pulled the trigger. There was only one gunshot, but it was louder than the dozens preceding it that night. Blood spouted from the back of Wolfram's head. A scrap of scalp flew away. Wolfram didn't move. A minute before, he had been the greatest threat that St. John's had ever seen. Now, he was muscles left slack. Still bones that no longer needed to carry the body's weight. A heart no longer needed to beat.

A choir of sirens sang out in the night. A fresh volley of flares burst overhead, bathing the waterfront in more of its creeping light. Frank swung open the cylinder of his revolver and checked its load. He didn't plan on firing it, but he didn't know what to do next. Checking his side arm was automatic for him. It was the only move he made that night that felt safe.

Chapter 29

Jack was driven to the hospital. At his insistence, Frank didn't follow. Instead, he went to fulfill his promise to break those bastards.

Three hours after the gun battle in St. John's Harbour, Frank stood on the stony shore of Conception Bay. He watched the bay's Seal Cove from an adjacent beach.

As much as he adjusted his binoculars' focus, he couldn't see the artillery guns that had been rushed onto the coastline, but he knew they were there. He and the other coast watchers standing near him had been informed that the army had towed a handful of guns from Signal Hill all the way to Conception Bay.

All he could see were the oversized waves breaking into white surf a moment before they vanished with the night's wind. The military had hidden those guns well.

At last, he saw the signal. A lone flare fired into the cloudy sky. With its glow, Frank searched the waters, looking for a periscope or some telltale sign of the submarine. He saw none and was beginning to believe that the captain of the U-boat had sensed something was wrong and had fled. Then, he watched a shape emerge from the quiet ocean. Like all sea monsters, it couldn't be seen in its entirety. Frank could make out its tower and the small line of its hull from the ocean spray blowing over the bow. He knew the submarine was moving fast and heading towards the shoreline.

The captain had not sensed the trap — the darkness that had helped hide a U-boat for so long now worked against it. The vessel clipped along the surface as quickly as it could to rendezvous with Wolfram's team.

Frank estimated that the U-boat was, at most, a couple of miles offshore. He held his breath, waited for what he knew was coming.

Another few seconds passed before the shore's spotlights were turned on. Their great beams shot forth from Seal Cove's beach into the roiling leaden waves.

Frank could clearly see the submarine now. The exposed U-boat was still charging towards the shore, with sailors frantically running past each other on its deck. On top of its tower, he could make out more men pushing each other to get down the hatch. He could only imagine what they were yelling.

That was when the shore's cluster of artillery guns fired from their hiding place. Most of the rounds from the first volley sent splashes of freezing water onto the panicking sailors. One round struck the U-boat amidships, just above the waterline. Frank was certain that the men who had been scrambling down the ladder a second earlier had been caught in the explosion.

Some of the sailors who had been on the deck were blown overboard. He thought he could see some bodies churning about in the submarine's wake.

He now had a better view of the submarine — it was illuminated by its own fire. Frank shifted his binoculars along the length of the U-boat. To his surprise, he saw a few silhouetted figures trying to get the vessel's 105 mm deck gun into action. A near-miss artillery round splashed down only feet from the U-boat's port side. It shot a stream of water skywards. When it cleared from the air, those courageous sailors were nowhere to be seen.

More searchlights and 4.7-inch, quick-firing guns from Bell Island added to the carnage. Frank had no doubts that the garrison on the island was eager to avenge the recent sinking of several iron ore ships.

The artillery guns had found their range, and the U-boat's length of two hundred and fifty feet made it an easy target. Another shell crashed into the vessel near the bow. A second blast followed, compounding the damage. Frank guessed the shell must have ruptured something explosive, like an ammunition store or a fuel tank.

He was certain the U-boat would crash-dive and try to escape. Yet, it only floated motionless in the water. He assumed it was so damaged that it couldn't make a break for the open ocean.

Not that an escape attempt would have helped the submarine. Flares and star shells were being sent off like the finale of a fireworks display. Frank could see a line of warships closing far behind the submarine. They closed the bay for any possible breakout.

Whether the submarine was still operational, or the Germans had detected the fleet of warships at its rear, the fight was finished. A sailor clambered out of the hatch and onto the tower's top. The frantic man waved a pole-mounted white flag so wildly that Frank was certain he would fall overboard.

The cheers of Allied servicemen could be heard from one end of the bay to the other. One soldier slapped Frank on the back and offered him a drink from his metal flask. Frank lowered his binoculars, and while he drank, he noticed that every house along the coast now had its lights on. Many citizens were streaming from their homes towards the beaches to see the commotion. Frank knew that they would soon piece together what had just transpired: An Allied victory was just won in the citizens' own backyard.

Epilogue

Frank crossed the street to the hostel's ruins. So many days had passed since he and Jack had first visited the site. Soot and piles of ash remained, putting up their resistance to the city's perpetual rainstorms. In his arms was a mixed bouquet of gerbera daisies wrapped in white paper and tied with a red ribbon. He wasn't sure if daisies were the choice flower for a memorial, but he felt they conveyed a soft sincerity that, unlike so many other things sincere, didn't overwhelm. He decided to wait until Jack arrived before he placed the flowers.

"Hey! Were you waiting long?" Jack called.

Frank watched his partner walking off the sidewalk and into the debris. Frank looked for any indication that Jack's hip wound had left him impaired but he saw none. In the sun's morning rays, Jack's red hair seemed to catch fire. His complexion, which Frank usually saw as hoggish, looked healthy and vibrant. His intense eyes, calm.

Jack easily crossed through the hostel's remains and sidestepped the smudged chimney. Frank again witnessed how light-footed his partner was.

Jack smiled and waved with his right hand. Bandages poked from underneath his coat's cuff. "Hey, how are you, b'y?" he said.

"All right. Good to see you up and around. How's the wrist?"

"All right. The doctor sounds hopeful. It was a lot better than it looked at first."

"How are you holding up against the onslaught?" Frank joked. "Managing all the attention okay?"

"Between the police investigation, the military investigation, and the bloody newsmen, I got people harassing me at all hours. Calling me up during my supper, showing up on my step before breakfast. Who do these people think they are?"

Frank nodded. He had been going through it too, and as charmed as the hotel staff were with having a celebrity staying with them, Frank was finding it a pain. Somehow the newspapers managed to make the event even more sensational than it had been. He supposed that was part of their job.

He and Jack were hailed as heroes worldwide. It was a great story about the two men's short-handed defence of St. John's Harbour and the defeat of a German U-boat. The locals were calling it the "Battle in the Bay." Frank's good looks gave him enough appeal that two casting agents had contacted him about minor movie parts. He wondered if his old girlfriend Joan would be jealous.

Jack's superiors discarded their earlier criticisms and concerns regarding his conduct. Any boundaries he may have overstepped were now seen as the small indiscretions of an overzealous policeman. His old rank was restored. He was no longer an acting sergeant — *Sergeant* Jack Fowler was reborn.

"I suppose with all that's been going on, you haven't had time to figure out what you're going to do when you get back to Canada," Jack said.

"I may stay with the military police. They offered a promotion. As well, I've been encouraged to run for public office in Ontario."

"You? A politician? Thank God Newfoundland and Canada are separate countries, that's all I can say."

Frank laughed. "And who knows? Maybe when I get back to Canada, they'll use me to recruit or to sell war bonds. And what about you, Jack? If you left the constabulary now, I don't think anyone would think less of you for it. What, with everything that happened and all."

"No, I'm too young to retire, and too old to start over in a new line of work. It's back to policing for me — as soon as the wound stops oozing and the stitches come out. I'll be restricted to light duties when I first get back. The surgeon said I can't lift any more than ten pounds for the first few months or I'll risk damaging my wrist further. But don't worry. I'll be able to get back to my full job again soon. I'm not hurt that bad, b'y."

Frank smiled. "I guess I should put these down," he said, and he lay the flowers in the cleanest spot he could find on the street-facing side of the ruins. Neither man spoke for a several seconds. For Frank, the silence was the only part of the ceremony that made it feel like a ceremony. It was a small thing — a small gust of ritual — but maybe that was enough.

Finally, Frank broke the quiet. He stretched his arms out and said, "So what about all of this? Is the constabulary still ready to declare the fire an accident?"

"Well, the investigation certainly has had new life breathed into it. The Chief has made the hostel fire a top priority. You wouldn't believe the number of guys he has working on it. It'll be a long time before they wrap it up. I think since they closed once, they don't want to come off looking hasty this time around. My guess is that at the end of the day, the fire will be called an act of war."

"Yeah," Frank said with a reassuring nod. "That would be one mystery closed."

"Yeah, one of many. I mean, what about their commanding officer, Wolfram? Why do you think he killed himself in the end? Was it pride?"

"Maybe national pride. I don't think a man like that thought too much about himself. Or maybe, in his picture of the world, that's what a failed commander does. If he doesn't get the job done and gets his men killed instead, then he does away with himself. He was one of the Old Guard. One of the Old German military elite left over from a time that, I think, may now have passed."

"So, what happened to the other German, Manfred?" Jack asked. "What did you Canadians do with him?"

"That's classified."

"Even from your partner?"

"Oh, to hell with it," Frank said. "What harm could there be in telling you now? After the smoke cleared over Conception Bay, and we got back to the station, I started placing a lot of phone calls to Ontario. It was very late by then, and I had to disturb the slumber of quite a few important people. But they changed their tune once they found out why I was calling. We worked out an agreement between the brass and Manfred."

"Which was?"

"In exchange for his co-operation, he'll get protection and a chance to start over in Canada — under heavy supervision of the Canadian authorities. Manfred agreed at once."

"Wouldn't you?"

"Damn right I would!" Frank laughed.

"They didn't tell me a thing after Manfred was removed from the constabulary's headquarters. I'm guessing he's living under an assumed name in the beautiful hamlet of God-Knows-Where, Canada." Frank turned to Jack and lightly punched his arm.

"Hey, you just called me your *partner*."

Jack paused and lit his cigarette, "I suppose I did," he said. He blew a long stream of smoke into the harbour sky. "I suppose I don't so much mind you being my partner, b'y. It seems it's all right with me."

Frank grinned at Jack's reluctant softening.

"What are you smiling at, Frank?"

"Oh nothing at all."

Jack clapped him on the shoulder and said, "So, when are you heading back to Canada? I'll drive you to the airport and see you off."

"I'm not ready to do the trip yet. Flying here was terrible, so I'm guessing the flight back would be just as bad. I'll stay here a while. See if I can get Newfoundland to join with my country. Then I can still be in Canada without needing to take a plane ride."

"Newfoundland join Canada? Don't be so foolish!"

Frank grinned. "Seriously, I'm going to stay in Newfoundland for a while longer. I've requested some vacation time."

"Oh yeah?"

"Yeah, your sister has asked me to stay for a couple of weeks, just to see the local sites. Beth kindly offered herself as a tour hostess."

"You and my sister together. What did I do to deserve this?"

"You think Beth could do better than me, eh?" Frank said between chuckles.

"Well b'y, she couldn't do any worse," Jack grumbled. He took a long draw from his cigarette. Frank didn't interrupt. He was savouring the moment too much.

Finally, Jack exhaled and said, "Well, Frank, she's a grown woman, so do as you will. But you're not bloody staying with me."

"That's all right, Jack," Frank said and grinned. "I've already made arrangements to stay at a nice affordable house on Gower Street."

Author's Note

This novel is a work of fiction and the events are all made up. It is, however, set in a real, historical Newfoundland — a country that was part of the front line during the Second World War. The capital city, St. John's, was a searing hotbed of activity in support of the Allied war effort. In its six years, the war brought more change to that city than it had seen in the previous twenty.

I hope this book has delighted its readers' imagination and has perhaps even inspired a desire in some to investigate this rich piece of Canadian history.

Acknowledgements

As always, Carolyn, my wife, gets the first thanks for helping me write this book. I'm also indebted to the many people who helped me with the book's research. It would have been impossible to revive the history unless aided by minds older and wiser than my own.

The good folks at Iguana Books were also vital to its development. Special thanks go to Iguana's Meghan Behse, Holly Warren, and Lee Parpart. Meghan's top-notch publishing skills were invaluable, and Holly's uncanny eye for small details made copy editing a breeze. We were lucky to have Lee join the team later in the publishing process. Her perspective made me re-think many problems that I thought I had resolved. Plus, Lee's Newfoundland roots helped to add authenticity to the story. Everyone at Iguana Books has my gratitude!

CPSIA information can be obtained
at www.ICGtesting.com
Printed in the USA
BVHW032349260319
543829BV00001B/65/P

9 781771 803083